THE LIGHTHOUSE

MICHAEL D. O'BRIEN

The Lighthouse

A novel

IGNATIUS PRESS   SAN FRANCISCO

The epigraph on page 5, taken from Psalm 107,
combines wording from the Douay-Rheims
and the New American Bible translations.

Cover art by Michael D. O'Brien

© 2020 by Ignatius Press, San Francisco
All rights reserved
ISBN 978-1-62164-366-1 (HB)
ISBN 978-1-64229-131-5 (eBook)
Library of Congress Control Number: 2020933463
Printed in the United States of America ∞

They that go down to the sea in ships, trading upon the waters, they see the works of the Lord and his wonders in the deep.

—Psalm 107:23–24

CONTENTS

The Island

The continent was limited and finite. Extending beyond it into the North Atlantic, as if by an afterthought or the remnant of a retreat, there was a solitary stone islet. Barely a hundred yards in diameter, it looked at first glance to be a barren place, though it was a nesting ground for seabirds and was visited by seals at times. Its forbidding circumference of black boulders had been hard pounded by the ocean for countless millennia, though above high-water mark a shallow turf rose to a promontory upon which stood a lighthouse.

The island was visibly connected to the mainland only at certain ebb tides, which revealed a narrow bar of packed sand and sea-rounded stones of various colors, a natural causeway extending for just under a mile. It was wide enough for three men to walk abreast upon, and perhaps at its driest it might have supported a motor vehicle with good tires, though in its long history this had never occurred, as no man had been willing to risk it, not even in the days of horse and cart, for the ebb was short and the sands unreliable.

Supplies were brought to the lighthouse twice yearly by boat from Brendan's Harbour, the port town that lay on the other side of the headland, miles to the south. They were offloaded when the sea was calm, onto a granite shelf, a natural quay that guarded a cove on the island's western side, the least vulnerable to the prevailing easterly winds. From there, the cartons of tinned food, the bags of flour and oatmeal, the jerry cans of diesel and kerosene, batteries and candles and sundry other items were carried up a gravel pathway to the keeper's clapboard cottage and the concrete tower, which were attached to each other by a work shed of rough timber and a weather-beaten outhouse.

Soaring twice as high as the cottage, the tower's massive white column was surmounted by a bright-red lantern room and its catwalk. Within the tower, each level was connected by an iron staircase. The ground floor was mainly storage, containing an assortment of cast-off items such as Argand wick lamps and components for the later Dalén lights, boxes of mantles, broken mirrors and lenses, overlarge dead radios, rusty gears and cranks, a heap of torn canvas, and crates of useless items such as rotted fishnets and moldy magazines that ranged from *Farmers' Almanac* to *Woodworking* and *Mechanics Illustrated*, all damp, stinking, and unreadable. On the floor above that, shelves stored the ranks of backup batteries and the beacon's replacement parts.

The staircase ended on the top floor, the circular watch room that contained the clockworks for rotating the beam, as well as a wooden map desk and a honeycomb shelf full of charts for the nearby waters. There was a separate desk for a VHF marine radio and an older shortwave radio. Beside it stood a low-magnification telescope on a tripod, its eye pointing out through the wide, double-paned windows that offered a view of the sea from north to southwest, where the headland was. A ladder led through a ceiling hatch to the catwalk.

The sole resident of the island had lived there for many years. He had first arrived as a youth, hired for a summer to assist the keeper, who was an old man in poor health. The boy had fallen in love with the place, had felt an injury in his soul gradually healing under the effects of distance and time and by the incessant rhythm of the surf, by the thrill of violent storms, and by the vast serenity of tranquil weather. On calm days he had bathed in the cold waves, had observed the comings and goings of wild-life, laughing at the seals' antics and wondering over his own laughter, so long silenced by life with human beings on the mainland.

For the first time in years the old man went to bed at night, as the boy kept the watch until dawn, reading from his bag of books while the keeper snored. The beacon's constant sweep and flash ceased to distract him after a week or so, becoming a background presence in his conscious-ness, though somewhere in his mind he was ever alert to any change in its rhythms, any warning that it might fail. Throughout that summer he and the keeper crossed paths over simple meals and when there were two-man tasks to be done, and most often during the warmest months, when the boy could not bear to miss what could be seen by daylight. He was vital, enthusiastic, interested in every-thing, and thus he chose to get by with little sleep.

The old man had not been difficult to live with, though he was generally uncommunicative. This, however, was to the boy's liking, for he himself was silent by nature. Attentive to whatever the keeper showed him, he had learned by imitation mainly; he asked questions sparingly and thought carefully about the gruff responses. In this way he had amassed a good deal of knowledge about maintenance of the beacon, about survival on a rock, and about sea dangers. The boy had also learned, without words, almost without thinking, that the passage of time was simultaneously swift and eternal. As the end of his employment approached he realized that he did not want to leave, that the thought of parting from the island was strangely painful.

Then the old man fell seriously ill, and the boy radioed to the mainland about it, and the next day a boat came and took the keeper away. The boat's captain had brought a telegram from the authorities who supervised the light-houses along the east coast, asking the boy to stay on temporarily, so that the light would not go out. And so he had stayed, and then the temporary position stretched into a year, and after that it became permanent. Because all responsibilities were now his, he learned more about VHF and shortwave, about the beacon's engineering, about quantities of fuel and the precise amounts of energy these produced, about using rations carefully, and about measuring time. He found satisfaction in accumulating the mastery of things.

His new life offered him numerous other pleasures:

The thrill of standing at the cliff face on the high end of the island, forty feet above the water, dressed in sou'wester and rubber boots, daring the thundering breakers to sweep him away, leaning into the gale-force winds as the soaring, frantic spray reached him and then withdrew.

The taste of his first cod, which he caught with line and baited hook and fried in canned butter. The taste of boiled seabird eggs. The taste of wild rose hips that he harvested from the bushes down by the cove.

The intoxicating aroma of crushed bayberry leaves from the bushes that fought for space beside the roses. The perfume of bonfires he made from driftwood brought along by the currents. The salt-scent borne to him across thousands of miles of ocean.

The abiding chorus of seagull cries. The beating pulse of the surf. The sight of sculpted seashells that lay scattered on the causeway after storms, which he gathered in his knapsack and set out in a row on his bedroom windowsill, where he could see them first thing at every waking. The antique fishing float, a blue glass sphere cast up on the cove's sandy beach, now reigning among the shells, its imperfections refracting amethyst light. The sloop with a red sail that skimmed past on an afternoon of pure sky and fresh winds, bearing children who waved at him long and eagerly as they diminished into the south. The puffins playing in the surf, more like children than children.

Most unexpected was the awakening of his powers of memory as lines from the books he read did not fade away, which was what they did on the mainland. And though at times he suffered from bad memories, they no longer tormented him, as if the tides protected him from all that had gone before. For the most part, he felt peace and the steady decline of fears save those of the natural kind: of falling into the sea, of freezing to death in winter, of tripping on a rock and fracturing his leg far from the radio, of the beacon breaking down. He also ceased to fear the inner turbulence that had been the habit of his childhood and youth, his loneliness, and his mistrust of human beings— though a quiet undertow of the mistrust remained. Against all odds, he had found a task in the world—and a home. He had been eighteen years old when he first came to the island, and here he had remained ever since.

His name was Ethan McQuarry. Rarely did he hear this name spoken by other human beings. It came to mind whenever it appeared on impersonal papers that arrived in the mail, the magazine subscriptions, the book club offerings, the documents sent regularly by the Canadian Coast Guard, which administered the lighthouses. There were disturbing moments when he could recall his name only after a few seconds of mental groping, a lapse caused by fatigue or by the mild illnesses that did occasionally happen to him. From time to time he worried that he might be slowly losing his sanity, but forced himself to shrug this off, for he was generally happy. Nor did he talk to himself, as so many people afflicted by isolation tended to do in stories. While it was true that he talked to the birds and other creatures, he knew they were incapable of responding with his language, and he did not supply the answers for them but let them be themselves, which was wonder enough. He spoke to the sea as well, and to the sky above it, and to the man-created things that moved through both mediums.

"A good journey to you," he would say, aloud, to a liner on the horizon heading out onto the open ocean. Or "Where are you going?" to a silver crucifix crossing from east to west in the dome above. And sometimes it was "Calm down, now!" shouted into the face of a rising gale, knowing he would be ignored. There were also conversations with characters in the novels he read: "I know you think it's hopeless, but it'll turn out all right in the end." Or "Don't shoot!" Or "If you were real, I would've looked after you."

There were times when he was overwhelmed by a quietude so profound that all noises ceased, and then he sensed the overarching *awakeness* of existence. He would have spoken with it, if he could, but there was nothing he could find within himself to say to it. It was enough to sense a presence in the world around him, a *listeningness* he called it, and to think about what it would mean if this were not there—though he had no precise words for it, and fell into silence.

Winter, spring, summer, autumn, the seasons turning and turning again, the patterns complex, not mechanical, often unpredictable, but giving a form to something larger, as the years slipped one into another. There had been dramatic events too. He was proudest of himself for preventing a catastrophe involving a cargo ship that had suffered electronic navigation failure. He had played a role in saving lesser vessels, usually in thick fog or in storms of terrifying power. Years passed between these incidents. He was not the Coast Guard as such, and he was an even further cry from Canadian Armed Forces Search and Rescue, though he spoke with both agencies now and then by radio, giving them remote assistance. He believed nevertheless that a keeper on this sort of coast should stand ever at the ready.

And thus from time to time he had used the rubber dinghy with its unreliable motor and had pulled distressed small-boaters into it, naïve tourists as well as unfortunate lobstermen caught in hard straits. He had fed them and given them blankets and his spare cots. The company was not unwelcome, but neither did he desire it, and they all yearned for the rescue boat to come quickly from the mainland. He wondered if their haste to get away was because he had grown taciturn with the passage of time and a little gruff in his own way, learned from the former keeper, though he strove to make small conversation. There was not much in his personality to offer a handhold, and, moreover, the castaways were distracted by their own immediate troubles. The rescue boat did eventually come, and the visitors departed. And though all of them were grateful for his help, none had left a thread that would connect him to their lives.

The dinghy had grown older with him, sprung leaks, resisted repairs, died. He was not unduly disappointed by this, for he had never liked the boat, which, when he tried to inflate it, flapped about like a kite at the worst possible moments. His repeated requests for a replacement had been unanswered until, finally, the supply ship brought him another rubber dinghy, which in turn caused him grief and steadily degenerated. He pleaded for a more solid craft, but this was met with unfulfilled promises. He wanted something substantial, a proper boat with a steady motor, with which he might save lives one day. And, without doubt, it would make his life easier in more mundane matters, sparing him the mile walk to shore and the five-mile walk along the coastal road to Brendan's Harbour.

In the early years of his time on the island, a diesel tank had been installed in the work shed that linked the cottage and tower, along with a generator for powering the beacon and recharging the backup batteries. He disliked its noise and so put it to rest during the day, turning on the machine only as afternoons waned or in the darkest weather when fogs or black storms obliterated the coastline. Twice a year his supplies continued to arrive by boat, but now, four times a year, a larger ship came and rocked in the swells offshore, pumping diesel into the tank through a long hose ferried onto the island.

Every summer, the inspector arrived by boat to see that all was shipshape with the beacon and that the keeper was still in fit condition to man it. He stayed for a day, gave a compliment, along with unnecessary pointers for improvements, which was in accord with his rank. For his part, Ethan wrote down the points on a pad of paper, intending to make suitable changes, or not, whichever seemed better. Invariably, the inspector brought with him a replacement keeper who would fill in while Ethan took his annual vacation on the mainland. Reluctantly, Ethan went. He carried his old backpack and a pup tent, a bit of cash, a book or two, and a map of the maritime provinces.

As the years accumulated, he came to appreciate the benefits of these brief separations, the pleasure of long strides, of routes that led somewhere, of the challenges presented by hills and valleys and harsh weather. Once, he rode a ferry to Prince Edward Island and walked its circumference, especially interested in its lighthouses. There were good conversations with other keepers. New Brunswick also had several beacons, and these helped fill out the map in Ethan's mind, the archipelago of sentinels standing watch at land's end. Many of the keepers were as chary of words as he, though some were garrulous, and all were content to stay where they were. When he returned to his island, he was always glad to be home. His replacements were always eager to leave.

Once every month or so, if the causeway was exposed and looked safe enough, he walked briskly to Brendan's Harbour. He might have taken the dinghy, of course, but something entirely instinctive in him disliked it; and his common sense reinforced the feeling, because the motor had a habit of failing after a mile or two of sputtering and gagging, regardless of the repairs he made, and he knew that it could easily gamble away his life if he were pulled out to open sea by the unpredictable currents.

The gap between high and low tides varied between six and seven hours, which gave him limited time to accomplish his tasks in town. The gap could be extended a little if he did not mind slogging knee-deep in water, though this was a risk, since the tide's water depth varied between five and six feet. Moreover, it was possible only between the advent of spring and late autumn, on days of relative calm. Long ago, he had cached a bicycle under a tarp on the mainland side of the strait, but it had rusted quickly. He bought another, and it had been stolen. Not wanting to waste any more money, he decided to walk from then on, which he knew was better for his health, since a man on an island as small as his could walk only in circles.

Unlike many coastal communities, the town seemed never to stop growing. More than a thousand people now lived there, and though the population of fishermen had dwindled due to poorer catches and economy, to failing health and retirement, with few younger men willing to take over, others had moved in. Older people from the cities wanted a rustic environment with the romance of the sea, a view out their picture windows and beaches to comb. There were foreigners buying up plots and building European-style luxury cottages south of town. There were artists living in restored fish shacks down by the wharf, hoping to survive and not worrying overmuch about whether they did or didn't. There were small shops that opened with optimism and closed with resignation, and seasonal restaurants hooking the trickle of tourist trade with fake décor and prepackaged seafood. There were also people who had left the harbor when they were young, for school or for jobs elsewhere, and were only now returning, middle-aged or older. And there were the abiding derelicts who frequented one or the other of two year-round bars.

Not many of the younger generation got married, and those who did had few children, if any, focusing instead on their lifestyles. There was a grade school, however, and those who graduated from it were bused to the high school in Glace Bay, a town of twenty thousand, farther north. Brendon's Harbor also had a bank, a post office, and a police station with two constables. The new regional hospital was small but competent, staffed mainly by out-of-towners. Some of the nurses were locals, but the doctors came from elsewhere, staying a year or two before heading off to better places. There were three churches, as there had always been, though their congregations were shrinking.

As the years passed, Ethan noticed that he recognized fewer faces than he had at the beginning, and by the same token an increasing number of residents failed to recognize him. He had never wanted acknowledgment, and thus he was at ease with the changing situation, merely finding it interesting the way so many people now walked past him, or through him, it seemed, as if he were invisible. This was to his liking, for it reinforced his understanding that his island and the lighthouse were the constants, solid and solitary, in an unstable world.

He made an effort at the sporadic sorties, which never quite became routine. Always he dressed up for these occasions, preparing for them by washing his socks and long johns in the kitchen sink the night before, hanging them on the cord clothesline he strung from hooks in the kitchen corners. Following a sponge bath, he donned his green hardware-store pants and a clean bush shirt, the offending holes hidden by his canvas jacket, and the whole topped off by his black fisherman's cap. On his feet he wore his battered hiking boots, for his rubber sea boots would have been too cumbersome for walking such a distance. As an afterthought, he sometimes shaved his face and gave his shaggy hair a trim with scissors, going blindly around the parts of his head that he could not see in the mirror, not much pleased by the final effect.

When in town, it was his habit to pick up his mail, deposit his paychecks in his bank account, visit the library, and hike toward home as fast as his feet would carry him, with a sack of new reading material on his back. His only real anxiety in life was the thought that someday he might not be able to beat the tides, and that he would be stranded on the mainland, leaving the lighthouse vulnerable. He knew that if worst came to worst, he could wait out two daylight tides, which would make him absent from his island for twelve to fourteen hours. But this was possible only in the best of conditions, during summer's long days and when the weather was calm and the causeway fairly exposed.

There were times when he did not leave the island for months on end, throughout the winter, of course, and in other seasons due to ill-fortuned tides or storms. Yet he was content with this, for the consequences of a wrecked ship or people drowning were far worse than overdue-book fines at the town library. Besides, the elderly librarian would sometimes waive the fines, depending on her mood, which was as variable as the sea's.

"Try to do better next time, Mr. McQuarry," she would scold with a look of impatience.

"I will, Mrs. Riley," he would reply with murmured diffidence, understanding that she needed her authority, her rights of rebuke, which would give way to benevolence at her own tide's turn, for he was, after all, the keeper.

"Mr. McQuarry, Mr. McQuarry," she would flutter toward him at his next visit, holding high a book. "A new acquisition! *Building Your Own Wooden Boat*! I've just catalogued it and have been saving it for you."

"Thank you very much, Mrs. Riley. That is so kind."

This is the way people are, he thought. *These are habits of speech, of manners and disposition. These are wounds and tempers. These are frail breakwaters that guard the harbor of the soul.*

And I too, he reminded himself, *am shaped by what life does to us.*

Though Ethan was still recognized as the keeper by many in town, he was not really known by anyone, and never had been. He was a symbol of sorts, or a walking landmark, because people understood his role and the terrible caprices of the weather and that he was the sort of man who saved lives. In the early years he had strained to make conversation with townsfolk, but realizing that he was no good at that kind of thing, he gave up and kept it simple from then on.

In those days, too, he would glance at the young women he passed on the street, yearn for them, and then turn his gaze in another direction. He had a general sense that he was good-looking, with a nice face that drew eyes to him, and a sturdy frame, balanced and taut with muscle. But he also knew that no one would wish to live with him on the island, not even in the bond of marriage, and that love would inevitably founder on the rocks and he would be left desolate. Moreover, his deepest passion was for the lighthouse, which had become life for him. Many of the young women had thickened and greyed over the years, and though they still nodded at him in recognition, they did not initiate conversation, nor did he.

I would have loved you forever, forever, he would think as he passed them with a lift of his cap, *though we would have broken each other's hearts.*

The postmistress kept a special carton for him behind her wicket, because there was often too much mail for his lobby box.

"More books and magazines than ever!" she would say, with a teasing tone. "How do you find time to read it all?"

Oh, you know how I find time, miss, for I am alone. And content to be so.

He would nod and mumble a meaningless reply.

Her remarks, her posture and eye contact were often coy, occasionally flirtatious, though not seriously so—just fishing expeditions on her part, or testing the waters. His consistent lack of response had not dissuaded her, and with the passage of time he had come to the conclusion that it was no more than her way of being feminine. It seemed to him, however, despite all her baiting and lavish cosmetics, that her manner was not in essence womanly. And he could not bring himself to respond from sheer physical attraction, knowing that the world was pain racked because so many people used each other for pleasure or for relief from loneliness, leaving them lonelier than ever.

No, it's not for me, that way.

The manager of the chandler's shop, an older man named Biggs, sold him rope and caulking and waterproof Irish sea boots, as well as assorted marine hardware, wrapping them up in brown parcels and twine as he offered bits of waterfront gossip, though he could never elicit any social barter from the keeper, leastways no personal items. He was a grey-haired man of hefty build, who had an unconscious habit of snapping his suspenders against his rotund belly. Over the years Ethan had noticed a pattern: the snapping was reserved for customers who steadfastly refrained from being drawn into Biggs's conspiratorial gossip sessions. It was absent when heads were put together and whispered smirks ensued. Though Ethan was invariably a recipient of snapping suspenders, he observed Biggs's idiosyncrasy with forbearance, knowing that he had idiosyncrasies of his own. What bothered him about the man was the cool, analytical eyes in a mask of sardonic amusement over the follies of the human race. Ethan did not trust such a face.

Nothing of myself would I tell you, sir, for it would be twisted as you traded it to other ears.

In contrast, there were artless, transparent faces about town, for instance the old men who sat perpetually on benches by the harbor's wharf, their weathered, honest eyes squinting at the horizon, pausing to peer at Ethan and wondering who he was—though they had once known who he was—as their minds lost memories like wash running down a deck and out through the scuppers.

There am I, a few years from now, he would remind himself. Then the unspoken salutation, *Take your ease, O steadfast men.*

These were men who had once been boys, and now a new generation had arrived, boys who would someday become men, racing past him on squealing, salt-rusted bicycles, shouting to him against the wind, "Hey, captain!"

He would wave back and think: *Speed well, lads, but seek the far horizons, be it land or sea.*

Then the bank people who welcomed him with professional warmth because he was thrifty and responsible, a long-standing client, very polite. And the grocery store clerks who never failed to offer cheery greetings, which may have been genuine and which he returned with a pleasant word or two. Also the manager, who on occasion strolled over to the checkout counter and stuffed into Ethan's sack, without charge, a package of cookies past the eat-by date—usually his favorite, shaped like maple leaves—or a plastic liter of milk, which cost an extortionist sum on Cape Breton Island.

Most important were the last remaining fishermen whom he happened upon at the dock or the hardware store. Unfailingly, they would tip their caps and engage him in mumbled exchanges about the weather. He would decline their offers of a cigarette or a sip from their flasks but was willing enough to spend a little time with them, for he admired their lives and felt sorrow over the declining fishery. Mostly he listened to their observations and philosophical thoughts, nodded his understanding, and had to hasten away because of the tides, an abrupt departure that they understood.

And no meeting lacked the ritual parting:

"Well, keep safe out there on the deep," he would say, his eyes as grey-blue as fathomless waters.

"Keep the light burning, boy," they would reply.

This had begun when he was a boy, in fact, and now that he was older he did not mind that they still called him "boy", or "son", and on occasion, "skipper".

Thus his life had slowly assumed its permanent form.

The Boat

The day did come when the sea cast a great gift upon his shore. It was a half-wrecked lifeboat, which he discovered wedged in the rocks after the fringe of a hurricane had passed. It must have fallen off the stern of a larger ship, not abandoned by survivors of a sinking, for there were no signs that it had been used; there were no oars and no motor on the stern plate. It was twenty-two feet long with a beam of about eight feet, open topped, lapstrake, and built of heavy planking. Most of its strakes on one side were staved in. The keel and bow beam were dented but otherwise undamaged.

As Ethan surveyed the boat, hands on hips, eyes soberly assessing every detail, he felt at first that it was beyond redemption. But it had once been beautiful, he saw, graceful in design, perfectly adapted to the humors of the sea, serene or enraged. It had been badly hurt, and he did not want to discard any hurt thing.

Thus he freed it by long labors, levering rocks apart with an iron bar, and then slowly winching it up from the shore with block and tackle, a few feet at a time.

How old was he then? Maybe late twenties? He looked a fair bit younger and regretted the fact, for age and experience seemed to him a more desirable state than that of youth. As a child and adolescent he had always been too short for his age. Though he had wasted untold desires for tallness, desperately willing his body to stretch upward, there had come a time when he had to admit that he was inexorably set for life at five feet four. Moreover, he had been cursed with a boyish face, which remained with him still—the face that in his native streets had attracted bullies who wanted an easy victim. They had learned that he was not so easy, that his compact physique and swift reactions overturned their assumptions without fail. Even so, resolved as he was to defend himself and others, he had never been mean, either in his thoughts or his actions, for he had decided early on that he would not become like them. In those years he had held fast to his composure, his dignity, as if clinging to the debris of a sinking ship—the shipwreck that his life had been from the moment he was born. Later, this had grown into a quiet disposition of integrity. Now, though he was a small man, he consoled himself with the truth that he was still uncommonly strong, and that this strength could be used for repairing what the world had damaged.

Year after year, his daylight hours were preoccupied with the boat. He was in no hurry, and he wanted the job to be done right. Working in the shed that linked the tower and the cottage, its double doors open wide for light, he was restoring its former glory by degrees. During the winters he eased off, but always with the return of spring he ached to get back into the shed. One whole summer was spent steaming and bending the planks he had shipped in as replacements for the broken strakes. Another summer, he built a forward deckhouse, so small that no more than a single man, or maybe a man and a half, could fit inside it. The following year he scraped the hull and repainted it white. The next winter brought too much snow, and due to staring at white-on-white for countless hours, he had learned that a stroke of color made anything greater than the sum of its parts. So when the warm weather returned again, he painted the hull's gunwales and the cabin's trim a brilliant red.

Throughout this long process he pondered what he might call the boat, for she needed a name, as all things need a name. Eventually he settled on *Puffin*. Practicing with pencil and eraser on broad sheets of paper—the backs of old charts—he wrote and rewrote the name in swirling calligraphy until he was satisfied that it was exactly as he wanted it. When the warm weather returned he duplicated the letters onto the stern and painted them red with meticulous attention. After the paint was dry he applied coats of spar varnish over it.

This precipitated another task, for it came to him that varnish would give added protection to the entire boat. So the remainder of the summer was devoted to coating her inside and out. That year, too, he hammered long copper sheeting to the lower hull, estimating where the waterline would be, once she was launched. And sealed it, though he wondered if the resins were more symbolic of protection than practical.

Looking ahead, Ethan plotted devices that would enable the relaunching of the boat, for she was far too heavy to push back down to the sea by his own strength. He drew plans for skids and winching that would assist gravity without letting the boat get out of control and destroying what he had so lovingly restored. He pored over catalogues and dreamed of the outboard motor he would order, to be delivered by the supply ship, maybe next year. Someday he would clamp it to the boat's butt plate and fire it up, and then he would do what he had never done before— steer his own craft outward into the unknown, guided by his growing knowledge, his eye, and his hand.

One autumn day a package of tools he had ordered arrived in the mail, containing a set of wood chisels wrapped in a leather pouch. The steel blades were straight edged or curved or V-shaped, various sizes for each, an array that would allow him to carve things, as well as to trim boards and rough timbers. He wanted a figurehead for the boat, and would use the green log that had drifted south from the forests of Quebec or Newfoundland and was now seasoning in the rafters of the shed. He did not yet know what the figure would be, though he was confident that in time it would become clear to him.

Another year passed as the log dried.

During the longer hours of night watch he would spend an hour or so scanning the shortwaves. Sometimes he picked up stations as far south as Boston and as far north as Reykjavik, and once, to his perplexity, a nonstop piece of music that was performed by oriental instruments and a chorus of women singing at a pitch higher than he had ever heard before. It had no beginning and it had no end. He presumed it was Chinese or Mongolian but was not sure. The traffic he listened to was mainly marine, though he also spoke with land-bound ham operators, exchanging information about the places where they lived. Now and then, one or another would call him to ask about coastal weather, usually during bad storms. The calls were never long, just checking in, distant people collecting entries for their logbooks. The simplicity of Ethan's life and his dearth of opinions was not conducive to dialogues.

On rare occasions he tried the small transistor radio in the cottage, looking for AM and FM stations that might play the quieter sort of music. There was not much to choose from, as the air was clogged with a nerve-racking array of frantic singing that whined or screeched. He liked classical, but the stations that specialized in it were few and the reception unstable.

Many a night he read through the watch, novels at times, practical engineering more often, and occasionally the Latin dictionary and grammar that he had bought at the library's discard sale. He also continued to work his way through his Shakespeare, a big book with small print, containing an oceanic chronicle of human nature. It became his habit to mouth certain lines that moved him, mysterious or fathomless yet implying something powerful.

There is a tide in the affairs of men, which taken at the flood, leads on to fortune. Omitted, all the voyage of their life is bound in shallows and in miseries. On such a full sea are we now afloat . . .

Wide-eyed, he devoured accounts written by explorers, and the stories of shipwrecked castaways. He memorized the poems of a man named Frost. Occasionally he jotted down small thoughts of his own in a notebook:

—Do I live in the shallows or on the brink of the deep? Both, I think. Does my position limit me or expand me?

—Whale plumes NNE this afternoon, about three miles out.

—Why do people hurt each other? What do they think they're doing when they do it? Protecting themselves, or fixing the world to make it safer, or punishing life for being imperfect?

—The height of the lamp in feet (h) must be sufficient to be seen by mariners before the ship reaches danger, according to the distance to the horizon in nautical miles (d). Minimum height is calculated by $d = 1.17h$. My light is okay, though I wish it was higher.

—Will this new Global Positioning System destroy lighthouses, make them redundant? Can you fall in love with a GPS? No, you can't. Is it beautiful? No, it isn't. And where are you when its battery dies? False dependency, false promises.

—Puffins lay only a single egg per season. The parents work very hard to guard it and feed the offspring once the egg has hatched. I wonder if the chicks realize how much it costs.

—Ideally, I should install an inboard motor, with a wheel and rudder. But that would reduce carry space in the boat, and I'd have to reconstruct the stern for driveshaft, etc. What is the comparable driving force, in reality, between inboard and outboard? I'll probably order an Evinrude 90 hp, maybe a Mercury. All outboards are horribly expensive, at least with my salary. The dinghy's 12 hp kicker is useless, never reliable, and now it's dead.

—A flock of small white ducks in the cove this morning. I've never seen this kind before. They stayed a couple of hours, diving for minnows or maybe just taking a rest, and then flew away. Need to buy a better bird book. Or check the library?

His mind was hungry for it all. He had not persisted in high school beyond grade ten, for he had been forced by abandonment and other circumstances to take to the bush, sweating and freezing in logging camps during two long winters, feeding the pulp and paper mills of mainland Nova Scotia and New Brunswick. In those days he ate much and thought little and wrestled with anger over his fate, though the money was a compensation. He saved it in a sock under his pillow, absorbing with an impassive face the mockery of his fellow jacks because he would not gamble or drink with them. One time his money was stolen, and the thief was never caught.

Much has been stolen from me, and I've learned what misery it makes. I will not be like that. I will work, and then I will build a place to live, far from people.

So he absorbed the loss and sighed and said nothing and returned to work. And from then on he guarded what he earned. After that came the summer wanderings, circling the coasts on foot with a pack and a tarp rolled on his back. He immersed himself in the vistas of the sea, the heights of the Cabot Trail, the beaches strewn with stones tumbled out of the roaring surf, ovals and spheres of different colors. One of them had been shaped like the planet earth, with swirls of storms circling the green continents, and though he loved it, he left it behind on another beach, for he could not carry a pack already overweighted with marvels. He would carry them in his mind, his memory.

There were, too, the occasional washes of beach glass and polished ceramic from old shipwrecks, man-made bits of crockery with painted designs on them, with no sharp edges. Once, he happened upon an enormous whale, decomposing on a pebbly strand, stripped by the gulls nearly to the bones. His nose clamped with thumb and finger against the stench, he examined it closely, astounded by the complicated simplicity of vertebrae. This was but one of many encounters in which awe and sadness became one.

He avoided Halifax, for it was a dark place in his mind. Its thieves and betrayers. The unknown man who had been his father, who had left him in the womb, giving the seed of life but not bestowing his name. His mother, who had often left him alone. The screaming and slaps and the alcohol. And afterward her crushing embraces and promises, her *sorry, sorry, sorry* sobbed again and again, before the cycle repeated itself. Then his withdrawal into silence, for he had learned while very young that promises were unreliable and that speech provoked incomprehension, misinterpretation, and at times, punishment.

And then her final departure, leaving him a note of explanation: *I'm going west. You're strong enough to make it now. Have a good life.* And in this definitive absence, after grief, after anger—*Well, at least she didn't kill me*—he had realized that despite all her faults he loved her, or pitied her, for pity is a form of love. Other boys and girls in the streets around him had experienced similar things, and while their sufferings varied, in essence it was the same:

I do not want you, they had been told. *I am not wanted,* they told themselves, and retold, though not with words. They had drifted into rage and violence, and manic laughter when in groups, to alcohol and drugs, and a few into prostitution. Feeling that they were worthless, they beat or humiliated weaker children, weaker youths, as if by asserting a little power they rose above their state. Ethan was sometimes tormented by them as a child, but he learned to repel such attacks with his fists. It was purely defensive, but there were occasions when he would hurl himself into harm's way by intervening in bullying sessions, rescuing younger or weaker children, taking the blows upon himself. Yet even as he fought the tormenters, he understood them, for he knew that their violence was against themselves. And after a time, as he grew in strength, they left him alone.

I will be different.

Later there was the girl he had loved, a nicer girl he met in his last year at school, who had taken from him his heart and his body, and then left him because he was too silent, too unsure, too bewildered by her moods that were so like his mother's. And shortly after that single moment of passion, furtive and frantic, the ecstasy too brief, he had carried his hurt and shame away with him into the bush.

Erratic as they were, his years in classrooms had given him a priceless gift: he had learned and remembered. Now in one school, now in another; as his mother had moved him from tenement to shanty to tenement, books were constant. In books he had come upon an unexpected solace, distraction from his more grievous thoughts. In books were promises of other ways to live, and though he did not know how he might live a better way, he now understood that it was possible. In books he found hints that pointed to an undiscovered key to life: turn the key, and the locked door of isolation would open. History. Geometry. Nature. The stories he happened upon: a snow goose, an old man and the sea, the little boats of Dunkirk, captains courageous.

Now, all these years later, he continued to stock his mind with interesting tales, with practical knowledge, and with vocabulary, learning and remembering. To learn is to survive. To learn is to come closer to finding the key. To learn is to feel the immensity of life, and its sweetness, even in its awe and sadness.

The following winter he carved the figurehead. He worked on it in the cottage. The cottage was three rooms only: the kitchen with its larger window facing the sea, its heavy shutters hooked back on the outside, the interior nearly filled with the little chrome table and its wooden chairs, the guttering oil heater, and the two-burner gas Primus for cooking, with a counter and sink and a stainless steel cistern that cached rainwater from the roof drains; the two other rooms with poor lighting and small windows, one room cramped with his bed and side table and lamp, the other crowded with boxes of canned food, bins of dry oatmeal and flour, spare camp cots folded up and leaning against the wall, waiting for emergency visitors, and the workbench that housed his numerous tools.

Day after day, he sat in a corner of the kitchen that he had cleared for the purpose, examining the lines and grain of the log, the log cut down to three feet high, braced temporarily by a square of timber he had bolted into its base. Tentatively at first, with uncertainty of hand, he tapped with wooden mallet and steel chisels, learning the art by trial and error. Though he suffered cuts and splinters, he saw that his droplets of blood absorbed by the wood were part of his investment in the boat, in the figurehead which represented it, for instinctively he knew that any abiding love would have a cost.

In short order there was a good smell in the room, replacing its customary atmosphere of rarely washed clothes, rarely washed man. The curl of a wood shaving doing what it should do as it parted from the main form, fulfilling hopes and estimations, gave Ethan joy—sometimes a laugh of pleasure.

Oh, now I see how you will be, what you will become. You will be beautiful, and I will love you always.

The shavings drifted onto the floor and were often left there for the night or a few days. Now and then he swept them up and saved them in an old burlap bag for the spring, when he would have his first bonfire of the season, and he would call to the puffins sporting in the surf and tell them about the great Puffin.

These are its feathers. These are the losses that make it what it will become.

As the future and the present sported in his mind, mingling, parting, and mingling again, the pleasure of anticipation grew.

The figurehead was indeed materializing as a puffin. It was not clear to Ethan how he knew the ways to shape it rightly. There were, of course, the nature books of birds he had looked at for hours, and whose images he had drawn on paper to get it right. But two dimensions was not three dimensions. He thought that perhaps all the images of the birds from books, and all the myriad times he had watched them at play, had sunk deep within him and merged and were now rising in a visible form.

The Atlantic puffin was a fine little fellow, stout and brave, rather stubby. And so Ethan was forced to adapt the shape of his carving, elongating the bird's body a little and using a swell on one of the log's sides as the breast. The splendid beak demanded finer work, and he saved it for last. When that was done, he let the carving stand on the table for a few weeks so that he might check for any disproportion that was not immediately obvious. Only on its backside did he leave it unrealistic, for it required a flat length, which he measured and grooved so that it would fit snug on the bow beam, eventually to be bolted there.

After checking time and again to make sure the groove fitted perfectly, he positioned the carving at the top of the beam and drilled three holes straight through the front of the body and deep into the beam, countersinking the holes so that the bolt head would be flush with the surface. He intended to use brass, but in the end he changed his mind and whittled hardwood pegs from a leftover plank of seasoned oak.

Using mail-order artists' paints, he set to work giving the bird the appearance of life. He painted it in the cottage, before installation, because the kitchen was the warmest, driest place. It was a delicate matter getting the black crown and pale grey cheek patches delineated, first with pencil, followed by long hours of brushing in the sections without infringing on their borders. The white belly and underparts were simple, the triangular eye patches and dark irises less so. He had made the legs and webbed feet stretch downward so that they did not stick out at right angles, and these he painted orange. But the most exacting challenge was to render the complex beak with its boldly marked striations of red, white, and black, its flanking strokes of yellow, and the orange cheek flash. When it was all done he sat back and gazed at it in wonder. It had come from him, and he did not quite understand how.

Weeks later the weather steadied, and one bright morning he slid the carving onto the bow beam, then inserted the wooden pegs. When they had been tapped in true, he coated them over with the colors that matched. And when he was sure it was dry, he varnished the bird, watching with a smile as the colors sprang to more vivid life and the white tones grew warmer.

Days of late spring arrived—and the return of the true puffins, a few of them making nests in the rocklet isles along the mainland shore, where the grassy tops offered hiddenness. Fewer still were willing to risk a nest so close to the tower and the presence of man, but there were some who dared. He gave them plenty of leeway as they courted and mated and laid eggs and raised their young. He delighted in watching their behavior through his binoculars. The males and females bore identical plumage and markings; the male was slightly larger. They plunged into the surf repeatedly and emerged with sprays of little fish in their beaks, which they inserted into the holes they had dug into the turf along the edge of the island. Before long their chicks emerged, looking a lot like their parents but lacking bright colors. They grew at an astounding rate. From time to time Ethan was able to crawl through the grass undetected, close to the puffins, and listen to their calls, which were a variety of *ooh-aaah* sounds that were very much like a baaing flock of sheep or a tiny growling chainsaw, which made him grin.

He liked to make small driftwood fires down on the cove's beach, when the wind was blowing away from their nests. He poured the bag of shavings onto the roaring flames, watching the wooden feathers catch fire and rise as smoke into the sky. And one morning when he went out to see the puffins, he found they were all gone.

That is their way. They depart from the land in silence, at night, and are seen no more until they return after years at sea.

The route from the work shed to the cove was about a hundred yards long. It was a good deal of distance for the boat to be winched, and there was little time or purpose for it, as autumn threatened to change to winter. The first sleet storms had already passed through, coating the tower with ice. After that, storms increased in frequency, though sometimes it was only a sprinkling of large white snowflakes blown sideways, sometimes strong wind and rain. Then came a sunny warm day or two, followed by more storms, increasing in intensity and duration. Once a gale-force wind sent the spray from breakers up the height of the island to glass its eastern side. The mainland now remained white. The launching of the *Puffin* would have to wait.

The boat was adequately sheltered in the shed, but Ethan took pains to cover her with a large tarp and secure it round and round with a hemp rope. He looked intently at the lumber pile beside her, and the various drift logs he had collected over the years, some still green with slippery bark. Sets of block and tackle dangled from the rafters, the pulley blocks large and heavy. The coils of rope would stretch out hundreds of feet, enough for the job, he estimated. He would have to keep a sharper eye on the water flowing past the island, since he needed more logs for rolling the boat downward to the sea.

I am almost forty, he thought. *Or near enough. Ten years I have given to this boat, and still she is not launched.*

Next year, then.

The Family

Ethan sat for a time at the kitchen table, sipping from a steaming mug of coffee, watching night fall over the whitecaps out on the sea and listening to the faint sound of the breakers. The sweep and flash of the beacon did its work faithfully.

The forlorn atmosphere in the room pressed upon him, a feeling that something, or someone, was missing. Gazing at his carving tools, folded neatly in their pouch on the countertop, he reminded himself to put them away in the workbench drawer in the other room. As he rose to do just that, his eye was caught by the pine log that tilted against a corner wall. After he had cut off a portion for the puffin carving, he had not taken the unused section out to the shed for storage but had kept it here in the kitchen for the aroma it gave.

He poured himself another cup from the pot simmering atop the oil heater. He sat down. He sipped more coffee and thought.

Why not? Yes, it would fill the hours in a good way. I will see if I can make another as fine as my puffin.

The log was about six feet high and nearly a foot in diameter. It had odd bulges and curves. It suggested a leaping porpoise, or perhaps an elongated whale standing upright on its tail. Maybe a thin bird, like a cormorant. Or, perhaps, a woman.

And so he made the woman. Months of labor she demanded of him. Love she asked of him, though gently,

38

without pressure, and like all men he was certain that he was courting *her*, beguiling *her*, though sometimes he would ruefully smile as he realized it was the other way around. He kept her clothed, though her body was womanly beneath the folds of her dress. He made mistakes with the chisel. Learned from them. Corrected them. How to cooperate with the grain to make a flow of line simulating cloth, implying fertile shapes. How to carve the small feet pressed together. Then the finer details of toes, collarbones, ears, the threads of hair, the definition of human eyelids, more complex than a puffin's. Splinters festered, were expelled or extracted with a pin. Blood was spilled and soaked into the wood.

Abiding love. It always costs, if it would endure.

And finally, when she was completed, or nearly so:

My wife.

The thought came unbidden into his mind. He did not like it, for it seemed not only foolish but a little demented. Even so, after hours of turning the problem over and over, it came to him that a man might look at a photograph of a lovely woman in a magazine and wish her for his wife, knowing that it was impossible. One might see a real person from a real family, soon to make another real family, and dream that the new one was his own, knowing it would never come to pass. So to imagine such a thing was not losing his sanity—it was to reflect on an ideal and to savor what might have been.

Of course, she was a woman without arms, this wife.

In the work shed he found some seasoned pine boughs, cut them to proper length with the bow saw, and brought them into the kitchen. He whittled oak pegs for the shoulder sockets, drilled their holes, then set to work on the bare curving arms that opened slightly apart from the body, reaching forward to enfold him. By then it was late

January, and not once since autumn had he been drawn to the mainland, not even by the lure of his impersonal Christmas mail or accumulating paychecks. He now lacked all perishable foods; tinned soups and stews and pan biscuits fried in the grease from canned bacon sufficed. Each day there was progress on the woman, sometimes minimal, sometimes a breakthrough when he saw what he should do, and did it.

Hello, he would say to her each morning when he returned to the cottage after a night in the tower. *I'm home from work now, and I'll make us breakfast.*

So far, she had not replied, no mental dialogues, which was a good sign, considering his niggling worry about his mind. He merely loved her, and she was content to receive that love. Sometimes he laughed at himself for all of this.

Then he tumbled onto his cot in the other room, and slept. In the afternoons he worked on the carving for a few hours before departing for the top floor of the tower, where he would monitor the sea, check for any signs that the beacon was having difficulties, listen to the conversations of others on the VHF, or make his weekly report to the authorities. Most of the night he was awake, vigilant and waiting. It was a peaceful time, and occasionally he thought of carrying his wife up the treacherous staircase to the third floor, so he might work on her there. But he decided not to risk it. One tumble, and months of labor could be lost. *Besides*, he reminded himself, *she is a presence in my home. She is waiting for me.*

In February the carving was complete. He sanded every surface with extreme care, using a grit that left no scratches. In March he painted her. Tan skin with a blush on the cheeks, rose lips not too gaudy, dark brown hair, a green–blue dress the color of the sea on his favorite kind of day. Her eyes needed an artist's skill, and he was no

40

artist, he knew. Nevertheless, he persisted, and after much effort at refining his brushstrokes, wiping off paint, and starting again, there came a day when she looked as real as life. He positioned her in the kitchen corner facing the outside door, so that she could greet him on his every return home.

She did indeed become a presence. Though she was not a living one, it was as if an inner imagining had escaped from his mind, or erupted from his heart's deepest longing, to take its solid place in the visible world. She never lost her dignity and composure. Her face was always compassionate and wise, her arms reaching for him. There were evenings when he came back down from the tower just to see her. To see if familiarity was dulling his emotions. To make sure she had not gone away, leaving a note.

He was a bit concerned about these feelings, their powers directed toward an inanimate object. It was dead wood, he knew. It was paint. It was an image, not reality.

And why do I need to tell myself this? he remonstrated.

This could become obsession, he said, warning himself. *This could become madness.*

But it did not, because he had books to distract him, and the minor crises connected to the sea's tempers, and the greater love of his life, the boat he had made, which was a different kind of passion.

Yet the woman, his wife, remained with him. And this led to the baby. Carving it was easier than making the previous two, for its face was simple, and all its limbs were enclosed within a cocoon. Painting it was simple too. White swaddling cloth, pink face, wisps of golden hair, the smile as if the child were grateful for existence, rosy apple cheeks, blue eyes. It was looking at him, very happy to know him.

Papa!

Yes? he said to the baby.

What is my name?

So a dialogue had begun. A worry, this. But not unpleasant, and sometimes rather funny—as long as he kept his grip on reality, he reminded himself.

I think we'll call you Ethan Junior, he told the baby after a few days had passed.

And Mama? What is her name?

Which sparked a more complicated series of doubts.

For now, Ethan, you can call her Mama. I'll call her Your Mother or My Wife.

Which seemed to satisfy the child, for he was pleased by simple things.

But, really, was this supposed to be the woman's child, and by implication his own child? Ha! No way! Nevertheless, it seemed to Ethan that the baby needed a family. So he began work on two rather spindly older children, a big brother and a big sister. He chipped out their rough shapes, with no delicate work, and cut four pine boughs in the shed for their arms.

By then it was late spring and the puffins had returned, so he left off carving for a time. Summer was near, and he remembered that during warmer weather visitors sometimes came to the island unannounced. He wrapped up the family in burlap bags and stored them in the other room, where he kept his tools and food.

Why are you hiding them? he asked himself.

Was it hiding? Or was it so private that he did not want people commenting, criticizing, praising, tittering, analyzing, gossiping?

The way they do. The way people are.

The inspector would be here next month, along with the vacation replacement. And what would that person get into during his absence? Would his privacy be respected?

After mulling it over, Ethan removed the family one by one to the work shed and installed the figures inside a big sea locker, a massive old storage cupboard seven feet high, eight feet wide, and three feet deep, made of two-inch pine planking. He closed its ancient cracked doors, padlocked its rusted hasp, and covered the whole with a tarp. Then he swept up the shavings scattered about the kitchen floor and saved them in a bag, and went out to the cliffs to spy on the puffins.

That spring, another surprise arrived on his island, appearing out of the immensity of the blue and taking up residence for a short while. It was a little covey of murre birds. They courted and mated on the rocks of the island's southern side, giving the puffin colony a wide berth. Their black coats with white underparts were similar, but in behavior they were very different. They produced harsh cackling calls and laid their large, sea-green, speckled eggs on bare rock, nurturing them there until hatching and maturity. The harshness of the "nest" astounded Ethan. How different it was from the puffin burrows lined with feathers and grass, and the off-white eggs with their flecks of grey and brown, and the way the puffins guarded their hatchlings under their wings. No such coddling for the murre chicks, it seemed, and yet somehow they survived. Before long the murres departed with their young ones, and never returned.

The inspector came and went, taking Ethan Senior with him on the boat, leaving the substitute keeper to look after things. Ethan was dropped off at Brendan's Harbour, where he dealt with his business matters, receiving a boxful of mail, doing his banking, and paying library fines. There were so many more unfinished tasks that he took a room in a bed-and-breakfast, one of the new ones where he was not known.

The town was too noisy at night, the lights too bright, the bed too soft, though the breakfast the landlady served him the next morning was the best meal he had had in many months, maybe years. She was a white-haired motherly sort of person who wore an apron over a dress, made her own soups and pies, had a kindly eye that had seen a lot of life's happy moments and its sorrows. He recognized her nature by sense—not through any experience of his own but from novels he had read over the years. She told him she had opened the "B and B" after her husband died out on the Grand Banks in a storm. His body was never found, his fishing boat just matchsticks washed up on Sable Island. But she had more than twenty grandchildren, twenty-one next month. With much pride of accomplishment, she served the coffee hot and rich with cream, the sausages and griddle cakes vying for plumpness, along with maple syrup and racks of buttered toast and jams she had made from the wild blueberries and strawberries she picked along the coast. She told him her name was Elsie Whitty, and recounted stories as if he were one of her own family. He listened, attentive, not interrupting, as if he were appreciating a long piece of music on the radio.

The next day Ethan popped several envelopes into the post office box, orders for books, artists' paints, and better brushes, and at the chandler's shop he put a down payment on an outboard motor for the *Puffin*. After that he walked out of town and commenced his annual walking tour.

This year he planned to go all the way around Cape Breton Highlands National Park, part of which he had explored while walking the Cabot Trail years ago. During that earlier excursion he had paid attention to beaches mostly, to the shells and skeletons and floats and the endless variety of colorful smooth stones, including the planets of the solar system cast up from the universe onto the shores of infinity.

Now, he would head west, traveling by bus partway. First he walked the twenty miles to Glace Bay, where he caught a little bus that took him beyond the city of Sydney, which he wished to avoid, and brought him across a sea arm just south of Bras d'Or and then onto the main part of Cape Breton. Arriving at the village of Saint Anns, he got off and began his northward journey on foot.

Following the coastal road, day after day, he camped in the forest at night and ate whenever he could at cafés in fishing villages and small ports. After Neil's Harbour, the trail looped around the upper end of the island, and then headed back south along its western coast. For much of the way his route hugged the shoreline. He stopped to comb every beach, regretting the loss of the stone he had found years ago, the spherical earth with green continents and swirling bone-white storms, hoping to find it again or one very like it. While he saw plenty of other marvels, never again did he find his missing planet.

Now and then he came upon small outpost enterprises where souvenirs were sold, folk-art paintings of boats and harbors, decorative nautical paraphernalia, and abundant wood carvings of seagulls. As he proceeded farther south these shops became more numerous. In places such as Chéticamp and Grand Étang and Saint Joseph, the tiny galleries and their work sheds out back displayed an intriguing variety of creations.

Unconcerned about privacy, wood-carvers chiseled and whittled away at a log or board, or were busy painting what was completed. Little boats, of course. Many little boats of various sizes, their hulls carved from a single piece, their colors applied with care, the threads of rigging accurate.

There were lifelike puffins and seagulls and cormorants, all well done, though the puffins were nowhere near as detailed as his own.

A good deal of whimsy was also in evidence. There were human figures, some life-size, doing homely island things: A portly lady, who looked very much like Elsie Whitty, cooked chowder in a giant wooden vat, beating a big codfish over the head with a ladle as it tried to leap out. In another piece, an astonished fisherman pulled the *Titanic* out of his net, and in yet another a six-foot-high pop singer dressed in lurid colors played his electric guitar, his torso a driftwood longbow, his mouth open wide in a silent musical wail. There was a chicken in goggles driving a motorcycle. There were fantastical fish looking more tropical than tropical, and birds of paradise that had not existed until someone made them.

More-sober creations were mixed with the fun: handmade sailing ships of great majesty, with complex rigging and under full canvas; small log cabins, one with a man and woman and child in the dooryard, a tiny ax in a chopping block, the clothing painted by a master minia-turist, cotton puffs rising from the chimney. Though most of these works were within the genre of the primitive, they were expressive and often curiously sophisticated.

At Margaree Harbour, Ethan turned inland, following a gentle river, and by various side roads his route took him higher into sparsely populated hill country. At one point along the way, he heard the baaing of sheep beyond a copse of old apple trees, and stopped to lean on a wood rail fence to listen. A flock of woolly sheep meandered out of the trees and came to a halt to stare at him. Then came a brown ram with impressive horns, and it was followed by a huge white dog that bounded over to Ethan and began barking at him. An assortment of goats was scattered across the meadow nearby. Then a young man strode out from behind a hawthorn hedge and waved. When he came up to Ethan, he doffed his cap and bid him a good morning.

Ethan for once decided to engage in actual conversation with a stranger.

"Those are unusual sheep," he said.

"They're Icelandic," said the farmer. "They're perfect for this climate and produce excellent wool. Though the wolves got two last spring, I'm sorry to say."

"You have wolves around here?"

"Oh yes. It's an interesting story. Until the causeway was built at Port Hastings, the island was fairly free of marauders—a few harmless bears, a few coyotes maybe. Then the wolves came over and interbred with coyotes. 'Coy-wolves', we call 'em. The strengths of both species combined, you see. Or maybe it's their worst qualities, as seen from the sheep's perspective."

Ethan smiled, noting the good vocabulary.

"But not dangerous to man," he said.

"They killed a woman hiker a couple of years ago. Now they rove the island constantly, never resting, never settling in any one place. Mainly they take down small game and livestock wherever they find it."

"The dog ..."

"Ah, the dog," said the man, looking down at the beast and stroking her head. She gazed at her master adoringly, sat on her haunches, and dribbled a lolling tongue. "She's a breed that's supposed to guard sheep. But this softie bonded with our children instead and just protects *them*."

"A good thing she did."

"Aye, a very good thing. We have two of her pups now, and I'm training them up to do the job right."

"You have a beautiful farm," said Ethan.

"Thank you," said the man, looking about. "Yes, it's beautiful. This place was first homesteaded a hundred and fifty years ago. It was a thriving farm once, great for sheep and cows, though not so good for crops, with our climate. The past forty years it's gone back to bush, the pastures shrinking to a remnant of what they once were."

"That's unfortunate."

The man nodded. "Claire and I bought it for a song five years ago, and we hope to spend the rest of our lives building it up again. And maybe the children will too. They love it as much as we do. I'm Roger, by the way."

They shook hands, and Ethan, somewhat depleted after so much discussion, shifted the pack on his back and made ready to leave. But the man extended an invitation to lunch in the family's home, and against his better judgment Ethan accepted.

Standing high at the edge of the pasture, the two-story house was clearly an aged veteran of many human generations. Its tin roof, bowing along the peak, spoke of heavy winters, and its whitewashed shingle siding had known storms in all seasons. It looked small on the outside but was larger on the inside. They were met at the kitchen door by the man's wife, Claire, a stunning beauty in jeans and bush shirt, cooking something on the woodstove. She welcomed Ethan warmly and plied him with questions about himself.

When he told them where he came from and what he did, the family crowded around, children popping into the room to hear more. There were four boys ranging from the eldest in his early teens to the youngest, about six years old, followed by a three-year-old girl. They were all vital personalities, each of them different in temperament but exhibiting the family radiance and keen intelligence. The girl was clearly everyone's darling, with shiny mischievous

48

eyes and tricks just waiting to jump out of her. The house was crammed with books and musical instruments hanging on the walls, mainly fiddles. For lunch, they served him fish chowder combined with buttered bread made by the wife. The fish had been caught by the boys, "in our own river", they bragged, for a branch of the Margaree passed through their land. The potatoes were homegrown, the mushrooms picked in the nearby woods. There was unceasing noise of the kind that is happy and peaceful.

After lunch, the children begged to take Ethan up the hill behind the house to show him the view from there. Their parents gave permission. The five young ones led the way out the back door and began to climb the slope behind the house, into a forest of older gnarled trees, including ancient apples bowed over with an abundance of unripe fruit. The path zigged and zagged through the woods, the route well beaten and bordered by thickets of knee-high grass and wildflowers.

As they proceeded at a leisurely pace, Ethan realized to his amusement that they were accompanied by a growing crowd of creatures. About a dozen red-and-black chickens clucked and kept up with them on either side, along with trains of peeping chicks and a frantic rooster scurrying back and forth across the path. Half a dozen domestic game hens followed, squawking and pecking at seeds, dragging their long speckled tails through the weeds. Eight goats, young and old, held close to the trail, as did the big white dog and two snowball puppies that harried the goats' ankles and received a few bored kicks. In the rearguard came three cats, orange, white, and calico, ambling along as if they had no interest whatsoever in the proceedings, but never turning aside.

It was quite a cavalcade. Ethan wondered what made the animals behave so, until he noticed the youngest boy scattering bits of grain that he pulled from his pockets. It did not explain everything, so he wondered if the procession was prompted more by the animals' curiosity. Or perhaps they knew they were family too.

At the top of a rise the path ended at a ramshackle gate made of cedar rails wired together. Beyond lay a pasture reverting to bush, with hawthorns sprouting up here and there alongside split apple trees with half their trunks lying on the ground. Two heavy workhorses came thumping over to the fence to nicker and blow through their nostrils, eager for the wizened last-year's apples the children now offered them.

The humans and goats climbed or leapt across the fence and made their way along the edge of pasture to the height of the hill, where the forest opened up and displayed the valley below. Excited, the children pointed out to Ethan the silver line of the river, the distant glimmer of the sea, the fields their father was reclaiming, and other points of interest. They stayed awhile and went back down by the way they had come, the cavalcade following.

Arriving at the house, Ethan thanked them all for their hospitality and made ready to leave with as little fuss as possible. But it seemed they were loath to see him go, wanted to ask a hundred more questions about being a lighthouse keeper, about daring rescues and "storms of the century". The older boys were especially shining-eyed with visions as they tried to imagine his life. The girl insisted, in her little bird voice, that they would all go and stay with him on his island. The parents made him promise to come and visit if he was ever back this way. Ethan said nothing more, and shook their hands before heading down the lane.

About a quarter mile farther along, he stopped by the side of the road, sat down on the grass, and put his face in his hands. Unable to explain to himself why he was so overcome with emotion, he dried his eyes, got up, and continued on his way.

The next day he reached Hunter's Mountain and Big Hill, and from there he turned due east and crossed over the sea arm onto the Louisbourg part of Cape Breton. By dusk of the day after that, he arrived at Brendan's Harbour.

He stayed at Elsie's place that night. While eating an enormous supper, as his belly dangerously distended with his first full meal in two weeks, he tried not to see her in his mind's eye hitting a great codfish over the head as it leapt out of a vat. He almost told her about the carving, but she seemed distracted, her eyes red, quietly going about her serving but initiating no conversation. He supposed she was worried about some private matter. In the morning, he ate another prodigious meal, paid his bill, and left.

At the chandlery he learned that his outboard motor had not yet arrived. Resigned to more waiting, he went down Shore Street to the post office to collect any additional mail that might have accumulated during his holiday. As he stepped aside from the wicket, the postmistress and the next customer began whispering to each other like two gossiping girls on a school playground. Pausing by the lobby entrance to make a cursory check of the mail, to see what could be trashed, snippets of their conversation came to him:

"Poor guy ... never gets any personal mail ..."

"Why don'tcha write him a love note, Betty, make his day?"

"Nice lookin' but not my type ..."

"... shorty ..."

"... loner ..."

"... never smiles ... never says a word ... I'd die of boredom ..."

So would I, thought Ethan as he went out the door, giving no sign that he had overheard.

As if he were wearing a sou'wester on his heart, he sloughed off their gossip and made his way to the grocery store, where he bought a case of condensed milk, for one of his luxuries was milk in his tea, and there was no cow to be seen in any quadrant. Doubly loaded now, he staggered down to the wharf, where he hired a small boat to take him to the island.

The morning was clear, the water rolling with lazy swell. As the boat rounded the headland and the tower appeared in the distance, Ethan felt the thrill of returning home. The captain carefully guided the boat into the little cove and kept the motor rumbling as Ethan leapt out onto the granite quay. After unloading his gear, he said good-bye and turned onto the path to the tower.

"Keep the light burning, boy," the captain shouted after him.

"Keep safe out there on the deep," Ethan called back.

The substitute keeper was more than glad to see him, reported no problems during his absence, and left on the same boat.

But the town had suffered a blow while he was away. A church had burned to the foundations in the middle of the night. It was one of three churches in Brendan's Harbour, the Catholic one, the weathered clapboard edifice he had sometimes noticed during his shore tasks, glancing at its steeple as he passed to and fro. It was on a street higher up from the shore, a few blocks from Elsie's place. In his mail he found flyers calling townsfolk to a public meeting that by then had already taken place. The insurance would not cover the costs of reconstruction, apparently, and various fundraising events were being proposed. He gave it no more thought.

A month later, on a day when the sea was more or less calm and the causeway open, he walked to town, and after his usual business he dropped in at Elsie's, hoping for a cup of tea and a slice of pie. He found her in the guest parlor, knitting a lime-green scarf, with a box of tissues stationed beside her rocking chair, her eyes still afflicted with some unnamed sorrow. She had been crying.

"Is something wrong, Elsie?" he asked as she put the knitting aside, preparing to get up to put the kettle on the stove.

"Well, Ethan, it's Saint Brendan's. We're having Mass in the school now, but it's not the same."

"The church that burned down, you mean?"

She nodded, and tears filled her eyes to the brim.

"I don't know why anyone would do such a thing," she said. Seeing his incomprehension, she explained, "The police say it was definitely arson. They found a gas can in the cellar. One of the old metal kind. And the lock on the back door into the sacristy was down there in the ashes too. It had been broken, and the fire didn't do that; it was someone with a crowbar did it."

Ethan said nothing.

"Thieves?" he asked.

"No, not thieves. The gold chalice was still there, badly scorched and dented. And plenty of coins from Saint Anthony's box. It was hatred, pure and simple."

"But why? Why would they do it?"

"I don't know. I just can't fathom that kind of stone-heartedness." She shook her head. "Not in the least."

"Will the church be rebuilt?"

She nodded. "They're hoping to start next month. Construction company from Glace Bay is going to do it. The insurance is settled now, and people around town have been generous too. The other pastors have been getting their people to donate. Our parish priest has a friend who's an architect up in Sydney, and he's doing the drawings for nothing. Father showed us the plans. The new church will be as close to the old one as possible."

"A replica."

"They called it that, and I'm glad for it, but it won't be the same."

Ethan tried to absorb this. He understood why people could grow attached to a familiar building, a place that meant something to them in terms of memories—weddings and funerals, he supposed.

Now the tears spilled down her round cheeks. She plucked a tissue from the box and wiped her eyes.

"I'm sore missing one thing above the rest," she said. "We're a fishermen's parish, you know. Saint Brendan's was built in the early 1800s—she's older than your lighthouse, Ethan, and that's old too. She was put up by volunteer labor, not by a construction company. The men of the sea built it themselves. And someone made a fishing boat, the kind they had at that time, maybe four, five feet long, hanging from the rafters over the center aisle. I always loved it. I loved it as a child, and I loved it as a grown woman. I was married there, and all my babies were baptized there. And when Norbert was lost ..."

She could say no more for a few moments.

"When they found the wreck on Sable Island and we had the memorial service, I looked up at the boat and I said to myself, 'Elsie, that's Norbert's boat now. He's up there on that deck, watching over you and the kids.'"

"The boat in the church?"

"That's right."

She smiled a little. "Of course, her proper name has always been *Star of the Sea*. But everyone I knew called her *Peter's Bark*, kind of a nickname, friendly like. And then she was *Norbert's Boat*, but only for me. I never told anyone about that."

She stopped herself and looked down at the knitting on her lap, rocked a little, and sighed.

"Now she's gone."

"I'm sorry," said Ethan.

Elsie took a deep breath. "Well, life goes on."

Rousing herself, she got up from her chair and toddled off to the kitchen.

"Tea?" she called to him.

"Yes, please."

"I'm outa fresh milk. Canned okay?"

"Yes. Thank you."

Throughout the remainder of summer and autumn, Ethan watched the puffins and seals, and was more observant of the water, now and then collecting errant logs pulled along by the currents. He completed the carving of his boy and girl, painted them until they were perfect. As winter got underway, he began work on the carving of a man who would become the father of his wooden family. He made him taller than the woman, which meant, Ethan understood, that this was himself he was re-creating, the form he would have preferred to be, if his nature or his genes or his diet, or whatever else is ladled out of the big cauldron of life, had been kinder. Nevertheless, like its creator, the man was young and handsome, broad shouldered, narrow waisted, with big strong arms and plenty of lean muscles under the shirt and wide bush pants. The face was copied from the shaving mirror, though rendered with a better haircut. He painted it as carefully as he had painted the woman. It was Ethan and not Ethan, which was disturbing.

For a few weeks he laid aside his chisels, content to look at the completed family crowding his kitchen as he sipped his coffee, glancing up from his book now and then, smiling occasionally over the accomplishment. They looked happy, the parents and children together, forever.

But something was missing. He did not know what it was exactly, and did not strain to find an easy answer, just waited and listened. And then an image formed in his mind. It took him three more months to make a second carving, which he completed by late winter, or the tentative spring that arrived before he knew it. It was another version of the man who was his wife's husband.

The young man carried a six-year-old boy on his shoulders, the boy's hands covering the man's eyes. Ethan had intended to portray it as a fun ride, a playful sojourn—a powerless little boy controlling a giant, navigating him through the world in a moment of glee. Instead, neither of the faces smiled, and the boy looked frightened. Ethan tried to make them smile, but the woodgrain fought him, and the chisel kept slipping, drawing his blood, so in the end he let it remain as it materialized—on its own volition it would seem.

Tidal Wash

On the island, warm-blooded human beings were few and far between. There were infrequent encounters with people needing help on the sea, but rescue was saving lives, demanding no engagement in relationships beyond the tasks at hand. Thus, Ethan's gift of himself to imperiled strangers was no more than the effort fundamental to his duty. There may have been people among them who would have liked to know him better, but his expressionless face and the impersonality of his courtesies prevented it.

Over the years, other kinds of visitors had come to his island, causeway walkers or small boaters curious about the lighthouse or about his way of life. There were never more than one or two a season, always arriving during the clement months. Sometimes years passed without anyone at all. These were not rescue situations but were, instead, unavoidable intrusions. They were like the disturbance of waters in a wake, he thought, or more accurately a tidal wash, the casting of inexplicable flotsam onto his beach.

Then came the summer—the year after the church was rebuilt—when such intrusions became unprecedented in number and oddness, converging like a mountain stream racing through a cleft in the rock, narrowing as it entered the gorge and hurling itself forward with greater velocity, dissolving time, disrupting the right proportion of his world. And with it came a growing apprehension.

These encounters all occurred within the space of six weeks.

The first of them occurred while Ethan was busy with his annual spying on the puffin hatchery. Lying on his belly with his binoculars trained on the nesting holes, he heard a raucous *bwah, bwah, bwah*—the foghorn blasts of a medium-scale boat, coming from down near the cove. It was a sunny day, and thus he concluded that someone was trying to catch his attention. He got up and went to see what it was about.

The boat tied up to the quay was an old one, a thirty-six-footer that he recognized from Brendan's Harbour. He did not know the captain, but the aging, cobalt-blue trawler was familiar, one of the many veterans of the once-prosperous fishing fleet. A man—the captain, he supposed—was standing on the granite slab and mooring the boat to an iron stake that Ethan had recently hammered into a crack.

Three small people gingerly climbed out of the boat's well and stood clumped together, waiting. Two of them were elderly people in conservative clothing, with caps and scarves and red umbrellas, which they held above their heads, presumably against the sun. The third appeared to be an adolescent of some kind, possibly female, wearing a black denim jacket, black mini-shorts, fluorescent green stockings that appeared to have been spray-painted onto her body, and black leather boots with silver studs. Her hair was electric blue and spiked. As Ethan proceeded down the path to the quay, the captain hailed him.

"These people are from Japan," he called. "Doing a bit of touristing, wanted to see a lighthouse up close, hired me to bring them out here. Hope it's okay."

"Well ..." said Ethan indecisively, arriving at the quay.

"They'll just stay a few minutes. Nice people ... er, well, the old folks are nice. Can you do it?"

"All right. I'll show them around."

Halting introductions were made. Ethan said hello to the visitors. The old people bowed and smiled. The teenager merely scowled and avoided eye contact. Out of her pocket she whipped what looked like a cell phone or some kind of musical player. She plugged its cords into her ears and made no response to Ethan's greeting.

"The girl's the translator," said the captain.

"Hurry up! No waste time!" said the girl in a voice that was something less than a shriek but more than fingernails scratching a blackboard. Both men shuddered.

Ethan thought she would have been a pretty young woman if it had not been for the scowl, the arrogant eyes, the overabundant eyeshadow, the black lipstick, and the rings in her nostrils and around the rims of her ears.

"The old folks don't speak English," said the captain. "Tokyo Rose here tells me they're her grandparents. Not too happy about it either."

"Very unhappy," said the girl. "An' I don't like *you*, boat man, stink like bad fish. An' I don't like this nowhere place. Drag me all over boring place—Anne of Green Gables garbage. Now make lighthouse—quick."

"Hoo-boy," said the captain with a droll look at Ethan. "Well, the money's good."

"I'll give them a tour," Ethan mumbled, turning back to the path and beckoning that the visitors should follow.

When they arrived at the tower, Ethan delivered a small speech about the lighthouse's age and purpose and the perils on this part of the coast. The girl translated his three-minute presentation in thirty seconds. The old people smiled again and said a few short responses in Japanese.

The girl translated into English, using a feigned New York City accent.

"They say, *very interesting*," the girl explained, rolling her eyes. "Like, they think it's real cool, man."

He took them to the edge of island, the windward side facing the Atlantic, hoping the puffins would not be too alarmed. He said a few more things. Again, the clipped translation lasted no more than seconds.

Thinking that he could now conduct the visitors back to the boat, Ethan led the way past the cottage and tower.

"They wanna go inside," said the girl.

"The stairs are rather unsafe, and—"

"Yeah, yeah, but this ol' lady, she say she really need to take a look. Just bottom, can't climb up take picture from top. Too sick. You gotta do it. She dying."

"Dying?"

"Die-*ing*. Like, she got the Fukushima thing."

"What is that?" Ethan asked.

"Fukushima, Fukushima," the girl fumed.

"I'm sorry," said Ethan. "I don't know what you mean."

"Like the *tsunami*?"

He shook his head.

"Like 2011 earthquake?" Delivered with a curdling tone that said, "Don't you know *anything*, idiot?"

"Atomic plants gone bad, *radiation* ..."

"Oh," said Ethan, still not understanding, and rattled by the girl's apparent hostility. He had a vague sense that Japanese culture was based on respect and reverence for family ties. He was confused by how starkly her manner seemed at odds with this. Then he recalled a few young people he had seen in Halifax, dressed like her, behaving like her, so perhaps it was some kind of universal break with the past. But why so much anger? So much disdain?

60

"She got cancer," the girl murmured, her eyes growing moist.

"I see," said Ethan. "Please give your grandparents my sympathies. I can show them the lighthouse."

"Not *all* lighthouse, just quick look. They wanna take picture."

The girl snapped a translation—more or less accurately, he supposed, because the old couple began nodding up and down with large smiles. Very pleased, very polite.

"*Hai, hai*," they said in unison.

"Uh, hello," said Ethan.

The girl was not interested in the quick look and decided to stay outside, leaning against the tower wall. As Ethan led the couple inside, she began checking her cell phone or miniature music machine or whatever it was, thumbing its keyboard, earbuds in place. As it turned out, the old couple wanted more than a quick look, and begged to climb the stairs, their words unintelligible but their meaning clear enough. So Ethan succumbed and pointed them upward, slapping the guard railings by way of instruction and taking the rear position to catch them if they fell. Ascending very slowly, they chattered with enthusiasm all the way up to the watch room. There, their excitement increased, and they spent some time staring at the ocean from the window, taking many photos of the vista and a few of Ethan. He got them looking into the telescope too, and by wonderful luck there was a good whale plume three miles out, a humpback, he thought, breaking the surface now and then.

Returning to the ground floor with careful steps and an anxious hold on the rails, they emerged from the tower. The girl was just as they had left her, wired and wishing she could be elsewhere. Now her mascara had dribbled black lines down her cheeks.

Ethan gazed into midspace for a moment, as if listening to something, then dashed into his cottage. He was soon back with a blue glass sphere in his hands, the fishing float he had found on the causeway years ago. He knew it was from Asia somewhere because of the oriental letters embossed on it, but he did not know the difference between the characters of one country and another. When he bowed to the woman and placed the sphere into her hands, her eyes lit up. The two old people bent over it and began chattering to each other and pointing out the characters.

Bypassing the girl, Ethan pointed to the sphere, swept his arms across the eastern horizon, and made wave motions with his hand. The two old people nodded emphatically.

"*Nihon*," said the man, and then placed a hand on his heart. "*Nihon*." His wife repeated the words and gesture.

"Japan," muttered the girl.

Ethan saw a number of possible meanings in the gesture. Were they trying to say that the sphere did indeed come from their homeland? Or that they too were like this fishing float that had crossed an ocean? Or that they would take his gift into their hearts and always remember him?

It seemed out of place to ask for clarification, and besides, he thought, the gesture was enough, the pleasure in their eyes ample reward.

After that came more smiles from the grandparents, along with a few words that he presumed was their thanks, which the girl declined to translate. Then it was down to the quay, where the boat's captain flicked a cigarette into the sea and helped the visitors to board. Ethan freed the mooring rope and tossed it to the man.

"Look after these old people," he said to the captain.

"Oh, I will. They're good folks. That girl, though ..." He shook his head, a corner of his mouth sagging into an expression of long-suffering or irony. "Didya have a nice time with the manga zombie?"

Ignorant of the man's meaning, Ethan said nothing. No further communication was possible, as the captain fired up the motor and reversed the boat out of the cove. The old people waved, beaming at Ethan. The girl kept her back turned resolutely to him, typing away at her machine.

Forgoing the sight of their departure over the water, he turned toward his island and climbed the path to the tower, thinking about the girl's tears.

The following week was seared in his memory by an invasion of people from a luxury yacht, ferried to the cove in two lifeboats that were not unlike his own in design, though made of fiberglass. It was late morning when they arrived, and Ethan first became aware of their presence on his island when he was awakened by their loud shouts and hoots of laughter. There were more than a dozen visitors all told. As he hastily dressed, he spied their activities through his bedroom window, and then the kitchen window. Most were running about yelling at each other hilariously and arguing over the best place for a picnic. Raucous music screeched and boomed. They settled on the windward side, where they spread blankets and unloaded wicker baskets and uncorked wine bottles. He hastened outside and walked into the midst of their festivities.

He would not have recognized the grimness of his expression, being inside himself, but the invaders instantly knew that he was unhappy. This seemed to have no great effect on them, though a few of the younger men clustered together preparing to make a united front. A potbellied man with silver hair swaggered over and declared the party's intentions to make a day of it.

Ethan politely objected, informing them that this was government property and that they had not asked permission to enter it.

"Yeah, well, we're taxpayers," said the swaggerer with a smirk, emanating power and entitlement. This was followed by laughter from the others, and a few pseudo-jovial taunts, such as "Hey, chill out, man!" and "Have a drink!" and "Teddy's a pal of the premier."

Teddy, clearly the entitlement man, turned his back on Ethan. As did everyone else. A few men in Speedos strutted about, taking photographs of the tower and the sea, while a couple of young women dropped their bikini tops, stretching their arms high and soaking up the sun like contented cats. All the rest were drinking from wine and beer bottles and eating salad from glass bowls.

"I will ask you to leave now," said Ethan, still polite but immovable.

This threw a pall over the party. People frowned, turned away from him again, and went on with their business.

Teddy slowly pivoted and faced Ethan, took a step forward, and pushed his face too close. Ethan's street instincts, long dormant, sprang to the fore, but he controlled himself.

"How would you like to lose your job?" the man murmured with a sneer.

"You have ten minutes to leave," Ethan said, without losing his composure. "If you're not gone by then, I will radio the Coast Guard and the RCMP."

"The Mounties? Try it. My brother-in-law's got a big desk in H Division, so back off, little man."

The words *little man* very nearly pushed Ethan to precipitous action, but he did not move, and nothing registered on his face other than resolve, a degree of intransigence that Teddy and the others were, perhaps, unfamiliar with.

"Ah, c'mon," someone said, "let's find another island."

"Ten minutes," said Ethan calmly and turned away toward the lighthouse. Up in the watch room, he observed from the window as they gathered their blankets and baskets, looking uniformly sour, making rude gestures at the tower. A few of them hurled empty bottles onto the rocks at the edge of the island. He gave them ten minutes, and then another five as a bonus, and finally went back down.

They were herding along the path to the cove when he emerged from the tower.

"Come back when you have permission," he called. "Bring the permission on paper, and you can have your picnic."

Teddy turned to Ethan and shouted, "Kiss your job good-bye, you little ——," concluding with a foul word.

Not replying, Ethan followed them to the brink of the slope leading down to their waiting boats, and stood with hands on hips, watching them impassively as they left. They boarded their yacht and got underway. Ethan heaved a sigh of relief, returned to his bed, and went back to sleep.

Later in the day, he spent a few hours picking up discarded food wrappers from the turf, and broken glass from the rocks.

This was followed eight days later by a more wholesome incident.

After a lunch of soda crackers and sardines, he headed out to the work shed and, as usual, glanced in the direction of the causeway to get a fix on the tides. No sand was visible, but it looked as if a boat was immobilized halfway to the mainland, run aground in the shallows. He went back into the cottage and fetched his binoculars to take a closer look.

Now he saw that the boaters were two young boys. They were up to their knees in water, no life jackets, straining with all their might to push the boat over the bar and into the deeper water on the other side. But she would not move. One of them, the smaller one, fell and struggled to stand upright again. He kept slipping and falling until the older one waded to him and got him standing again. With alarm, Ethan noted that the propeller was kicking up wash—the motor was still running. Not a good idea, he thought—in fact, a really bad idea. He raced down to the shore and splashed as fast as he could along the causeway.

They did not see him approaching, and were still straining to push the boat forward, a futile effort, for the causeway, though completely covered with water, sloped upward. He noticed that the boat's name was painted on the side with amateurish letters: *The Purloined Peanut.*

"Hello!" he shouted above the roar of the motor, reaching over and cutting the throttle.

Startled, they straightened and regarded him with open, guileless faces.

"Hullo," they said in unison.

"I'm the lighthouse keeper."

"I'm Hugh," said the older boy, about thirteen years of age, soaked to the waist. "This is my brother Matthias." Matthias, soaked to the neck, appeared to be three years younger. Ethan saw plainly that these were good manly fellows.

"Having some trouble?" he asked.

"We're stuck," said the older one.

"We're *castaways*," said the younger, emphatically.

"Well," said Ethan, "I don't want to tell you what to do. It's your boat, lads, and it's up to you. But you're not castaways, not in any way you look at it. The tide's coming in, so you could sit here an hour or two until your *Peanut* floats."

They smiled, pleased that he acknowledged their boat had an identity.

"Then you could go forward across the bar and be on your way," said Ethan.

"That's a long time to wait," said the older boy, uncertainly.

"Not so long," said Ethan. "Time's different out here. But it depends on where you're going. You wouldn't want to be out here at night."

"We weren't going anywhere special," said the younger one.

"Yes, we were," said the older. "We thought maybe Glace Bay."

"That's a few hours north," Ethan said. "A long voyage, and you wouldn't get there until dark. Do your parents know you're out here?"

"Mum 'n' Dad said we could go along the shore as long as we get back before sunset. We're staying at the cottage in Brendan's Harbour."

"Well, you wouldn't be home by sunset if you went to Glace Bay."

Their faces fell.

Ethan looked closely at their boat, a scruffy shiplap affair, its motor probably older than the boys' parents. He had often seen young people paddling colorful plastic kayaks near the mainland, and adults in tougher sea kayaks farther out, but he now wondered why anyone would permit children this young to venture out on the ocean in a craft like this. It was likely that the parents had instructed them to stay close to the shore, and the boys had interpreted the word *close* rather loosely.

He said, "The other thing we could do is push the *Peanut* back out the way you came in."

The boys nodded. "That would work," said one. "Yeah," said the other.

"So, let's do it. But where will you go after that?"

They shrugged.

"It's best to have a plan," said Ethan.

Clearly, they had no plan at all.

"You're on an expedition, aren't you?"

They nodded, brightening, eagerness restored to their faces.

"It's just a suggestion, but I know a little island—a rock, really—a mile and a half north of here. Wreck Isle, I call it."

He had visited the islet a couple of times in the rubber dinghy, years ago, before it quit on him for good.

"There's an old wreck on the bottom," Ethan explained. "A sailing ship from a hundred years ago. Most of it's rotted, but you can see the beams still, like a whale's rib cage. If the water's calm, you can look down into the depths and see fish swimming in and out of the ribs. Tommy cod and striped bass. I've seen grilse there too."

Ethan glanced into their boat. Fishing rods and tackle boxes.

"You could catch some. Grilse are very good eating, a kind of salmon. Take one home to your mother for supper."

So it was decided. No question about it—a shipwreck and fishing!

First, Ethan made them put on their life jackets. He helped the younger boy into the boat and instructed him to sit on the stern seat, his weight lifting the bow a little. Then he and the older boy pushed hard on the bow and inched her stern-first out of the shallows. It was tough going at first, as they had run her aground yards up the flank of the causeway. With painful slowness the hull scraped over sand and pebbles, but the water was a little higher now, and this, added to a good deal of effort, got her floating again. The older boy clambered over the side and crawled to the stern, preparing to pull the starter cord.

"A couple of thoughts, lads," said Ethan. "First thing, you shouldn't get out of your boat with the motor running. And *never* try pushing her stern with the motor running. The propeller could cut you badly. Okay?"

They nodded.

"Second, when you're passing through unknown waters, you need a spotter at the bow. That way you can see rocks or sandbars before they jump out and bite you on the nose."

They smiled, and again nodded. The younger one moved to the bow.

"And don't take off those life vests under any circumstances, except maybe if you're cooking that grilse over a campfire—on dry land."

They laughed.

"All right, I'll push you off now," said Ethan. "Reverse your way out a good stretch, then slowly circle out of this bay and around my island and head north. You can pick up speed then; there's no sand on the other side. Keep going, and you should reach Wreck Isle within half an hour."

"Thanks, thanks!" they both shouted before firing up their motor and throttling it down to a purr.

"Be careful," Ethan shouted back, after a glance at his wristwatch. "With the tide coming in, the isle becomes less visible. At high tide it's underwater. Keep a sharp lookout."

"We will!"

After further reminding them to avoid the open sea and to head back to the harbor within a couple of hours, he watched them go, pondering that he had never had a brother or close friend, but glad that they did. When they rounded his island and disappeared from view, he took note that the water was halfway up his shins. At high tide it would be well over his head. The boys would do fine. He turned and sloshed toward home.

In the hottest days of summer, once or twice a month, he rewarded himself with a full bath in the cove. It was a mile from the mainland, too far for eyes to see him, and after a quick check of the water north and south, he felt sure that no surprises would arrive by boat from any direction. He stripped down to the buff and waded in, leaving his clothes and a towel in a pile on the dry sand. Here on the leeward there was little wind, and in the shallows the water was sun warmed. He soaped himself thoroughly, rinsing by swimming this way and that off the mouth of the cove, and then he floated on his back, his body soaking up the light. He had just walked out onto the beach, shaking himself like a wet dog, when he cast a glance toward the mainland and spotted a human figure walking deliberately toward his island along the causeway—only minutes away. Hastily, he dried his body with the towel and scrambled into his clothes.

He had just completed this task and was slipping his feet into boots when the figure arrived at the end of the causeway, just where it linked to the north end of the cove, no more than a stone's throw from where he stood. The figure now materialized as a young woman—or youngish, he thought. As she approached, he noted her jeans and light windbreaker, the backpack on her shoulders, and a set of binoculars dangling on a strap about her neck. The binoculars gave him a moment's pause.

"Hello," she said, her face friendly—quite a lovely face.

"Hello," he replied, cordially but without enthusiasm.

"I'm sorry to disturb you," she said. "Are you the lighthouse keeper?"

He nodded in the affirmative.

"My name's Catherine MacInnis," she said, offering her hand and delivering a firm shake.

"Ethan McQuarry."

"I'm hiking the coastal road," she explained. "I saw the sandbar and just decided on a whim to give it a try. I hope you don't mind."

He shook his head.

"I won't stay long. Would it be possible for me to go up to the lighthouse and look at the ocean from there? I'm afraid I'm one of those odd types who stalk birds and seascapes."

She smiled, self-deprecating with no loss of confidence, though without any hint of the presumption he had experienced with the loud invaders from the luxury yacht.

"The puffins nest here," he said. "They're gone now."

He led the way up the path and took her beyond the cottage to the brink of the eastern rim of the island, where the breeze was stronger. His hair dried quickly, lashing about. Hers blew wildly in every direction, her eyes shining with some kind of hunger for the vista, a flush on her cheeks. He thought she was very beautiful. When his heart began pounding harder, he wondered if she could hear it. He swallowed and hoped she had not noticed.

To distract her, and himself, he showed her the puffins' nest holes and spoke a little about their ways.

Then came silence. She seemed to be comfortable with this, content merely to gaze.

"I've seen whales out there in the northeast," Ethan said, pointing. "I don't know all the species—from here, you just see them breaking. I've spotted humpbacks and pilots and minke from time to time."

She nodded but did not reply.

"Once, a blue whale. The largest mammal ever to have lived on earth, they say."

"It's a wonderful place to live," she observed. "You must be very happy here."

She turned and looked directly into his eyes, and he realized that she had asked a question.

"I am," he said, nodding somberly.

There was not much more to be said. He half hoped that she would now take her leave, allowing his unruly emotions to subside. The other half of him longed for her to stay.

"May I have a cup of tea?" she asked, withdrawing a thermos from her pack. "I've walked quite a distance without a break. Then I'll be on my way; I won't take any more of your time."

"That's fine," he said with a nod, feeling foolish. "Do you have any food for your lunch?"

"I have sandwiches, a few energy bars."

"I could fry you some Spam," he suggested. And instantly regretted the blurting, the forwardness.

She laughed. It was a delightful laugh, soft as honey, without mockery.

"No thank you, Mr. McQuarry."

They sat down on the grass. She poured tea into the cap of her thermos, and sipped from it. He kept his eyes on the horizon.

"Where are you from?" Ethan asked.

"Halifax. And you?"

"I'm from Halifax too," he said, realizing after it was out of his mouth that a cloud had passed over his voice, a downturn of tone. Yes, born and raised there. But had he ever been *from* there?

"Where are you going?" he asked.

"I'm hiking all around the coast of Cape Breton."

"I did that once," he said. "There's a lot to see. On the beaches, you feel you're almost inside the roaring surf, and you find things the waves cast up. Stones like you never saw before."

She smiled. "I'm going to visit every one of them."

"There are wolves."

"Yes, I've heard. I'll be careful."

He looked at her doubtfully.

She caught his worry, pondered it a moment, and then went on:

"I've lived what you might call a sheltered life, you see. I'm majoring in music. Concert piano. Full scholarship. I have the best mum and dad in the world, brothers and sisters who are my closest friends. So much love. So much ... safety. I wanted just to set off into the unknown, let the road take me, and even when the road runs out, I'll let the unexpected carry me farther." She paused and added, tentatively, "I mean, let God take me where he wants, so I can meet people he wants me to meet."

Which Ethan absorbed, thinking about it, finding it an alien concept.

"Do you believe in God?" she asked.

He had to think about this. It was too big a question, and too fraught with the potential for misunderstanding. So he weighed it a little, as much as he was able. And murmured, "I don't know."

She accepted that, saying nothing, though her gaze upon him was a fond one, with a hint of concern.

"An old poet once wrote that no man is an island," she said.

73

He nodded solemnly. Knew it was true. Knew also that he did not want it to be true. That he earnestly wished himself to be an island—and pretty much was one.

"This is so intrusive of me," she said apologetically. "I'm sorry."

"No need to be sorry," he said, slowly raising his eyes to meet hers. "It's a good question. It's like the sea, really. The world is like the sea. No, it's more as if everything that exists is the sea. The world, this planet, is the island. I'm not sure what I mean by that—it's just a feeling I get sometimes. Even this island here, my small island, is connected to the mainland by the causeway. At high tide the water's over your head. Most of the time the causeway's invisible. Even at some low tides it's still awash, especially in bad weather, storms, gales."

"You're saying you have to believe the causeway is there, at times like that?"

"Yes," he said, still looking at her directly, wondering at his overflow of words, and equally at the way she seemed to understand what he was saying.

"It's a kind of faith, isn't it, Mr. McQuarry."

"Maybe it's like that. A dangerous faith, though. After strong tides or storms, you find the sands have shifted. Or you lose track of time, and you're cut off."

"But there's something bigger than us—us humans. We'll never master all of it. I think that's what we're meant to learn."

"We can master a part of it."

"That's true," she agreed.

Now Ethan was yearning with all his being that the conversation would not end. That she would stay—and stay and stay.

He heard his voice trembling as he said, "Sometimes I feel a listening all around me."

"As if someone is listening to you, even when you're alone?"

"Yes. Someone good, someone with me. Or some *thing*. I don't know what it is, and I don't have any words to describe it. It's like an *awakeness* in the world. Do I sound crazy to you?"

"No, you sound very sane," she said with a smile.

"Well, people living alone do go crazy sometimes, hear things, start talking to people who aren't there."

"Oh my, I do that all the time. Sounds like we're both crazy—or else we're both sane. If I had to choose which interpretation, I'd stick with sane."

He laughed. It had been a long time since he had laughed. He didn't know why he had laughed, but it didn't matter, it felt so good. Now she was laughing too, which made it even better.

"I could show you the boat I'm rebuilding," he said.

"I'd love to see it."

So he opened up the work shed and escorted her around the *Puffin*, pointing out this and that detail, explaining, talking more than he had to anyone in years.

"She's beautiful," she said. "She's very, very beautiful."

She remarked in passing on the fine calligraphy on the stern, and stood still by the puffin figurehead. Her eyes grew moist as she examined every detail.

"Did you carve this?" she asked at last.

"Yes."

Mysteriously she made no comment; there was no praise. Just a brimming of her eyes.

He did not understand this—no, not at all. But her reaction didn't seem to be distaste. Indeed, just as he was leading her out of the shed, she stopped and went back to the boat, rose on tiptoes, and kissed the puffin's head.

Dumbfounded, he waited for her outside.

"I'd better go now," she said, glancing toward the causeway. "Is it still open?"

He checked his wristwatch. "You have just enough time. Unless ..."

She may or may not have guessed what he had been about to say. He had wanted to tell her that she could stay the night, that he had a spare cot; that he could make her a meal; that he would respect her completely, that she was in no danger from him, alone with him; and that the road to the next habitation was a long and desolate one.

"I should go," she said.

"I'll walk you to the shore."

They went down the path to the cove and then onto the causeway, which was thinning.

"It's a mile," Ethan said. "I'll walk you halfway. Just in case."

So they walked in silence, and in his mind's eye he had his arm linked with hers, or around her shoulders, protecting her from wolves, from the world, and above all from the humans who prowled out there in the dark. She made no objections when he kept walking alongside her the rest of the way, and then up the banks to the road.

They stopped and faced each other. They shook hands. She looked him in the eyes. His habit of dropping his eyes was discarded. He tried to say something but did not. He could not. He had no pattern in his mind for this kind of thing, no memory or model or language.

She seemed to understand.

She smiled at him and then turned and walked away. He stood on the road looking after her until she was no more than a brushstroke on the horizon. She went over a hillock between grassy dunes and was gone.

He nearly ran after her. Instead, looking back at the causeway, he saw it rapidly disappearing, and decided to run to the island. He made it home, wet to his knees.

He wanted to write her a letter. To invite her to visit again. To tell her more things about the sea and the sky and the deep waters of his thoughts—things he had never told anyone. But where would he send the letter? Why had he neglected to ask for her address? There were easily a thousand girls named Catherine MacInnis in Halifax.

Ethan consoled himself with the possibility that she might come back this way on the return part of her venture. Or, if the people from the yacht succeeded in getting him fired, he would go to Halifax and search for her. He waited and waited, and dreamed and dreamed, but she did not return. And for some reason or other, he was not fired. He never heard another word about the clash with the picnickers. And life resumed.

Save Us from Peril

Not long after, a week or two maybe, on a day of bruised sky with storm clouds low in the east, Ethan happened to be scanning the horizon from the watch room window and noticed a small fishing boat rising and falling on the incoming swells. It was a quarter mile south of the island in the direction of Brendan's Harbour. The anchor line was out. No larger than a distant mote, a man sat in the stern, hunched over, probably baiting hooks.

Ethan ignored it, but he checked again twenty minutes later, his curiosity aroused, since it was not a good spot for fishing and none of the local men ever bothered to try their luck there. Moreover, the storm front was closer, looking like black plums about to split and disgorge their contents. The wind was now blowing the swells into rougher waves. He moved his telescope and looked through it at the boat. To his astonishment he saw the boatman wrapping chains around his body. This made no sense whatsoever. He became genuinely alarmed when the man wrapped more lengths of chain around the outboard motor and bent over it. He appeared to be twisting something in a rhythmic pattern, and it looked very much like he was unscrewing the stern clamps. It took a moment for Ethan to realize that he was uncoupling the motor from the boat.

He rattled down the iron staircase, taking two and three steps at a time, and then shot out of the tower and across the turf at top speed. Arriving at the quay, he kicked off his shoes, stripped off his clothes down to his underwear, and dove into the water. The water was cold but not freezing, though the shock of it nearly stunned him. Rallying, he forced his body to move, kicking and thrashing, pushing his limbs and his lungs to the limit. It seemed to take forever, but at one point he paused to gasp for more breath and saw that he was closing the gap. The wind was at his back, and a current was helping. Again he swam, breaking his strokes only long enough to see that the motor was now skewed sideways, probably with one clamp fully off and the other ready to let go.

"Stop!" Ethan yelled, but the man either could not hear him or had decided to ignore him.

Now he pushed beyond his limits and arrived, nearly depleted, at the boat's gunwale. The old man, seeing him, turned the screw at a faster rate, frantic, wild-eyed, his teeth grinding in fury.

Panting, Ethan pulled himself up and over the side and sprawled into the boat, grabbing the chains wrapped around the old man, and yanking him away from the motor.

The old man staggered and lost his balance, falling backward and hitting the side of his head against a gunwale. After sliding into the boat's well, he groaned and lay still, unconscious. Or he may have been drunk, for there were liquor bottles rolling about in the open bilge. As quickly as possible, Ethan unwrapped the chains from the old man's body and then stepped to the stern and lifted the outboard upward. He needed three or four arms to do what was needed but somehow managed to tighten the single functioning clamp. With that, he was freed to unwrap the chains from the motor. Leaving them in a pile beside him, he straightened the motor and braced it with his arms, feeling blindly for the other clamp. When he found it, he hurriedly tightened it, and then lowered the stem and propeller into operational position and went back to look

79

at the old man. He was bleeding from a scalp wound, and there was a dark swelling on his forehead.

"Hospital, hospital," murmured Ethan. He made an effort to stop the bleeding by binding the man's head with rags he found in the seat locker. The rags were not clean, but the blood flow eased off. That done, he winched up the anchor chain, shipped the anchor, and fired the motor. It took only a moment to steer the boat around and get it moving toward the headland and Brendan's Harbour.

As the boat raced along, the bow bounced dangerously and the spray increased. Now Ethan was thoroughly chilled, and his teeth began to chatter. He slowed the motor and left it rumbling in idle, long enough to check the cabin for blankets or clothing, anything to shield himself and the old man from the windchill. There were no blankets aboard and no clothing save a workman's pair of coveralls hanging on a hook in the cabin. They were ripped and oil stained, but he had no choice, slipping hastily into the tattered garment. They were bib coveralls with straps that left his shoulders and arms exposed, offering little protection from the wind, but they were better than nothing. A pair of rubber boots lay broken in a corner, their tops slashed down to ankle length, heels cracked, the lining wet and stinking of fish. Ethan pulled them onto his feet and staggered back to the stern seat. He revved the motor to a steady roar and raced onward into the south. As he pushed it to maximum endurance the bouncing grew worse, and the spray reached all the way back and soaked him thoroughly. He rounded the headland shortly after, steering straight for the harbor.

Easing the boat toward the wharf, Ethan yelled to three fishermen loafing about.

"I have a hurt man here!" he called. They jumped up off their fish crates and hastened to meet him by a bollard.

One tied the bow line, and two others pulled the rear gunwale to the wood.

"This is Skillsaw Hurley's boat," said one.

"And that's Skillsaw," said the other, pointing to the prone body. "What happened?"

"He fell and banged his head hard," said Ethan.

The three men looked at each other.

"Drunk," said one of them.

"Yup, drunk," affirmed another.

"Drunk as a skunk and out in a boat on a day like this," said the third. "A guy who'd cut off his fingers, he's gonna someday cut off his own head."

Ethan interrupted. "There's a lot of bleeding, maybe a concussion. He needs to get to the hospital."

No one had a cell phone to call the town ambulance, and it was too far to carry Hurley physically to BH Regional. Between the four of them they were able to get his limp body out of the boat. One man ran to get his pickup truck and backed it down onto the wharf; then they loaded Hurley into the box. Ethan hopped up beside him and rode all the way to the hospital. At the entrance, a nurse and intern took over, transferred Hurley onto a gurney, and wheeled him into Emergency.

Ethan went in and sat down in the ER waiting room. His wet hair was in strings, and his borrowed clothes, such as they were, were dripping a pool of water about his feet. His body began shivering uncontrollably, and his teeth continued to chatter. Noticing this, a nurse brought him a blanket, and soon after a cup of sugary coffee. She wanted to check Ethan's vital signs, but he refused, saying, "No, no, I'm fine, thank you."

A couple of hours later, a different ER nurse came out to the waiting room and told him that Mr. Hurley had been placed in the intensive care unit; he was not out of danger.

"Can I go see him?" Ethan asked.

She hesitated, then said, "All right, if you stay only a few minutes. I don't think Esau has any family, and probably no friends to speak of. You rescued him, so I guess we'll call you a friend for the records."

She led him back through a maze of beds surrounded by curtains and into a hallway leading to the main ward. It was a small hospital, and they were there in a minute. The nurse left.

Hurley appeared to be sleeping. His head was bandaged, and his bare forearm was needled, attached by intravenous tube to a bag of transparent liquid. Ethan drew up a chair and sat down beside the old man.

He waited there for a time, listening to bells and electronic beeping and the scurrying of feet in the hallway outside. He watched the old man's chest rising and falling, his twitching blue lips, the hollow cheeks bristling, unshaven, the left hand missing three fingers. The terrible vulnerability of a life—the age and the self-neglect.

This the way we are, he thought.

He saw again the chains wrapped around the bootless ankles and the hanging motor. Was it an accident? Clearly not. No one alone in a boat would deliberately tie himself up in chains and then wrap them around an outboard and loosen its clamps, locking himself into certain death. If the old man had not been interrupted, he would have turned the screw a few more times, freeing the motor to drop away, dragging him to the bottom.

Staring at the floor, brow furrowed, Ethan was still trying to imagine why Skillsaw—rather, Esau—would do such a thing, when he looked up and saw the old man's eyes upon him.

"Where am I?" Hurley croaked.

"Hospital. Brendan's Harbour."

Hurley spat a word so crude it took Ethan aback, though he had heard plenty in his life.

They stared at each other until Ethan grew tired of it and said:

"Why would you want to kill yourself?"

"It was an accident," the old man growled.

"That was no accident."

"Who are you anyway? Police?"

"I'm the lighthouse keeper. I found you and brought you in."

"Well, good for you. You're a hero. Don't you call the cops on me, 'cause I ain't gonna let nobody send me to the loony bin. And I need a drink."

There was nothing to say to that, so Ethan asked again:

"Why did you do it?"

"Ah, no reason. It was just time to check out."

Ethan continued to sit, staring at the man, wanting to go, though he couldn't. And couldn't say why he couldn't.

"You can leave now," said Hurley. "Have a nice day."

"I'm not leaving."

"Tough guy, eh?"

"I'm not leaving. And you're going to tell me why you tried to kill yourself."

"Lots of good reasons."

"Give me one."

"None o' your business."

"You made it my business. I had to swim out to your boat. It was a long way, and the water was cold. I untied you and stopped your bleeding. I got your motor hooked up again, and then I brought you here. That's about half a day of my life. Probably a case of bronchitis too."

"Don't try t' guilt me out. It won't work."

Ethan coughed. "Maybe pneumonia, if it takes hold. A little explanation would be appropriate."

"*Appropriate.* There's a five-dollar word. You're a smart fellow, aren't you?"

"Not so smart. But I'm wondering why."

"Nice guy saves town drunk. Hero goes home to his happy life. Bad Boy Skillsaw goes back to the bar."

But even as he said it, Hurley averted his eyes and kept them averted. Beneath the bitterness, the mask of cynicism, there was a measureless grief.

Ethan was not a demonstrative person, neither a toucher nor a hugger, mainly because there had never been anyone who had stayed around long enough to show him how it was done—or how to receive it. Now, tentatively, he reached out and patted Hurley on the shoulder.

"Get yer hands off me!" the old man snarled.

"I'm sorry."

"Nobody touches me. I been touched before. I know what it's all about."

Tears began leaking out of one eye, then the other.

Ethan had no idea what this might mean, so he waited. Time stretched painfully long, then it slowed, and Ethan felt the eternalness he sometimes experienced while gazing at the sea. A sort of peace, an inner stilling.

Hurley turned his head and met Ethan's eyes.

"Back then, I told myself I'm not a bad person," he said.

"I don't think you're a bad person," mumbled Ethan.

"You understand nothing. Let me finish my story."

Ethan nodded. "Please, go ahead."

"Gimme ten dollars, and I'll tell you an *appropriate* story."

"I don't have ten dollars with me."

"Ten dollars buys a good bottle o' wine or a jug of bad rum, like home-still Newfy Screech. Ever drink screech?"

Ethan shook his head.

"Interesting. So now you know."

"Now I know what?"

"My life ain't worth ten dollars. Or maybe I'm saying it's worth *only* ten dollars, but nobody's got the cash to spare."

"I don't understand, Mr. Hurley."

Hurley snorted. "*Mister* Hurley, is it? My, you're respectful. Polite. A nice man you are, sure enough. You're one o' the good guys, not one o' the bad guys, like me."

"Are you a bad guy? I don't think so."

"Well, not in the beginning, maybe. It starts when you think you're not the kind who does bad things. Then, little by little, so quiet, so slow you hardly notice it, like a lamprey hooking onto a salmon, sucking out its life without being noticed, you do small wrongs that get bigger and bigger, and more of them. First you're standing on dry land watching the tide come in. You can hardly see it change. It looks harmless. Then before you know it your feet are wet, and soon your legs. And then you're swimming for your life, because you told yourself that you couldn't drown—not you—'cause you're the good guy."

"Mr. Hurley," said Ethan, his voice soothing, trying to calm him, reaching out to pull the blanket up around the trembling unshaven neck. With his free hand the old man batted Ethan away.

"Evil," he croaked.

"What evil?" Ethan asked.

"You're sinking and your head is full o' darkness, but you keep saying to yourself, 'This is right; this is good.' But you know deep inside yourself that wrong isn't right and right isn't wrong, so you make yourself blinder, do more evil because evil was done to you and life owes you."

"I don't understand," said Ethan, wondering what the man had done. Some foolishness committed when he was drunk, stealing lobster pots?

"Then you start hating anyone who says different. You hate them and kill them in your head, like the rage of dark angels burning inside you, and all the while you think *you're* the righteous one, you're the good guy saving the world from people who give other people pain. I don't mean the abusers; may they rot in hell. I mean the ordinary folk who you hate just for being themselves, for being good. I could hate you," he concluded. "You're the kind I could really hate."

At which point Ethan began to realize that the old man was like those kids he had known on the streets of Halifax when he was young. The mean ones, the bullies who were hurting themselves as much as they hurt others.

"I don't think you hate me," he said. "And I don't hate you."

"Well, stick around a while and hear me out. Y'see, it's like this: without knowing how you got there, you pick up a can o' gasoline and a box o' matches, get yourself a crowbar, and in the middle of the night you burn down their house."

"What?" murmured Ethan, his heart beating harder.

"I did it," Hurley rasped. "I was the one."

"What house did you burn down?"

"God's house."

"Why?"

"Already told you in a roundabout way, but you're too dumb to figure it out. I burned it down because God don't live there no more. Because there's bad fish in that net. Rotting from the head down. Like me, rotting from the head down. But I ain't no hypocrite, so I put an end to it."

And tried to put an end to yourself too, thought Ethan.

Hurley said nothing more, and when he fell asleep again, Ethan got up and left the hospital. Down at the main wharf on the harbor front, he checked to make sure the boat was still secured. It was, and Ethan asked a man to keep an eye on it until Hurley was discharged. Wanting to think about what had happened, he decided to walk home rather than hire a boat to take him. There was a lot to think about and he needed time to weigh everything he had learned. Should he call the police? Should he leave well enough alone? Should he go back to the hospital in a day or so and urge the old man to turn himself in?

Though he walked briskly, and even jogged a good part of the way, his thin, damp clothes—his borrowed clothes—were insufficient for warmth. By the time he reached the causeway, he found that it was rapidly being closed over by the incoming tide. Now he ran, and in the last hundred yards he was sloshing knee-deep in water. His coughing grew worse.

He did indeed develop bronchitis, and spent a few days in bed, though he still dragged his aching body up the tower staircase each night, barking and hacking through the hours until dawn. It did not turn into pneumonia, however, and the cough eventually subsided and sputtered out to nothing. When he was able, he sat outside on the warm grass with his back to the tower, soaking in the June sun, his body still weak but his strength returning.

Three weeks after his rescue of Esau Hurley, he made the effort to walk to Brendan's Harbour for mail and supplies. At the hospital, he inquired about the old man, only to learn that he had died the week before—a brain hemorrhage.

At Elsie's place he was greeted warmly and forced to eat a meal, though he was not hungry. Over tea, Elsie sat down at the table with him and said that she had heard about his rescuing Esau Hurley, that he had had to swim a fair ways to do it.

"That was brave," she said, and he was at a loss for a reply.

"You need a real boat," she cautioned him with a look of maternal scolding.

"I'm working on it, Elsie," he said, and she probed no further.

"It's too bad about Esau," she went on. "Too bad. Poor boy. Poor, poor boy. I knew him as a lad, you know. We were in school together. Then his father died, lost in a storm, and his mother not long after from cancer of the pancreas, which they say is almost impossible to beat. He was sent away to an orphanage up in the city, no family of his own to take him in, no one else willing to take him. My parents wanted to, but our house was always bursting at the seams, and never enough money to feed us right. But we made it through.

"Well, he came back a young man, so good-looking it made your heart skip a beat, and smarter than the rest of us. But he had no anchor—maybe no anchor inside himself. He wasn't in very good shape then, nor since. Drinking a lot at the time, which was the beginning of his troubles; he was never able to kick it. Went off to Sydney and worked in a sawmill for a while, lost three fingers there."

"Is that why they call him Skillsaw?" Ethan asked.

"Some hereabouts call him Skillsaw, making a joke of it, saying it takes a lot of skill to deliberately cut off your own fingers."

"Deliberately?" Ethan said with a frown, disbelieving what she said.

"He got ten thousand dollars from the company compensation, a fortune to him at the time. When he came back to Brendan's Harbour, he got to drinking hard and told someone in the bar that he'd tried to cut off *one* finger, left hand, because he's right-handed, you see, and that would have been ten thousand right there. But the saw jumped and took three from him. Made no difference to the company. Ten thousand's all he got." Elsie sighed and shook her head. "Must be forty or more years ago. But people never forget."

"What has he been doing ever since?"

"Fishing a little, collecting unemployment, maybe some welfare too. Getting into fights at the bar. Something happened to him up there, I think."

Up there?

"At the mill?" Ethan asked.

"No, not the mill. Before that, when he was a youngster."

"The orphanage, you mean?"

She nodded and blushed, and a weary grief filled her eyes.

Ethan pondered, remembering everything Esau Hurley had told him through implication or insinuation.

Elsie shook herself and went on:

"He had a lovely funeral at Saint Brendan's, though. Not many came, but a few of the women and me got together to sing hymns, and Father offered a beautiful Mass, and let the cost of the burial plot go. Someone made a coffin. We've put our pennies together and we're getting a headstone made, rose granite. We got his birth year right too. There weren't no documents in the old fish shack where he lived, but we found his baptismal certificate in the parish records. It was a sad death after a sad life. But you never know. Father went down to the hospital after he heard about the accident. Spent hours with him, heard his confession, held his hand when he died."

"His confession?" Ethan asked, not sure what this meant.

"The last rites, you know. Must have been at least sixty years of cargo to unload. I think Esau's happier now. I hope so. I pray for it."

"I hope he's happier too," Ethan echoed.

Elsie tilted her head back and closed her eyes. Hand on breast, she opened her mouth and began to sing in a warbling voice:

> O Christ! Whose voice the waters heard
> And hushed their raging at Thy word,
> Who walkedst on the foaming deep,
> And calm amidst its rage didst sleep;
> Oh, hear us when we cry to Thee,
> For those in peril on the sea!

Elsie's delivery was theatrical and full of tears, but it came straight from the heart. Ethan was moved. No one had ever sung to him before.

Walking back home to the island, he decided that he would never reveal what he knew about the arson. Telling the truth would not bring the old church back, and neither would it bring Esau Hurley back. If anything, it would make matters worse, giving the town more fuel for contempt.

As he pondered the events of the summer so far, Ethan grew amazed, in retrospect, at the sheer number of strange encounters—all within six weeks. He now wondered if Esau was the tipping point of those several incidents, one that could bring about a significant change in his life—unwanted, threatening change. The sequence of visitors played and replayed in his mind, as if there were a vast inarticulate urgency in the convergence. Had it shown him anything, really? Was there a meaning in it? Was there something he should learn from it? Or was it merely a case of the world becoming a busier place? Would the influx become a persistent pattern, increasing in volume and frequency?

He could not imagine what there was to be gained by racking his brain for answers to these questions, but they would not leave him alone. From time to time he walked to the edge of the island and sat down on the turf with his legs dangling over the rocks, and there he gazed for a while at the incoming waves, listening, waiting for the return of equilibrium.

Nothing came to him by way of explanation. Nothing at all. And finally, one day when the sun was setting behind him, he concluded that human affairs were as random as the sea's debris. He got up, turned away from the ocean, and trod slowly back toward the lighthouse with renewed conviction that he was at his best when he was alone. Solitude was peace. Interruptions were, in a sense, a kind of combat, an invasion.

The Visitor

On an afternoon in the first week of July, Ethan awoke, yawned, rubbed his eyes, and looked out the kitchen window to check the weather. It was a fair day, with high cirrus clouds, light chop on the sea. He went outside and walked the circumference of the island, which was his habit in summer, to get fresh air and a bit of exercise. As he rounded the west side, he noticed a boat beaching on the cove below. Wondering if the *Peanut* had returned, he sauntered over to the edge of the turf only to learn that it was not the boys' boat. This one was longer, aluminum, with a big kicker on the stern.

Another visitor, thought Ethan as he watched a figure making its way up the path toward the lighthouse— a young man, it looked like. When he spotted Ethan, he waved.

He was a tall, solidly built fellow, with a face lit up by a friendly grin—a face that was closer to boy than man. When they met at the top of the path, the visitor stuck out his hand and delivered a solid handshake.

"Hello," he said with a forthright look. "I'm Ross Campbell."

"I'm Ethan McQuarry."

"You're the lighthouse keeper?"

"I am. How can I help you?"

"No help needed, sir. I'm in marine biology and was just meandering along the coast, bit of a holiday, seeing what I could see. I don't want to intrude."

No, but you did stop.

The thought was not meant unkindly, though Ethan did wonder how long the interruption would take.

"The tower's awesome, quite old by the looks of her," said the boy. "Actually, I'm interested in where the puffins are nesting along the coast of Cape Breton. I'm kind of infatuated with puffins."

With that, the situation changed.

"Would you care to come in for a cup of tea?" Ethan asked. "I'm fond of puffins myself."

"Hey, a cup of tea would be great."

In the cottage kitchen Ethan invited the visitor to sit down, and he set a kettle to boil on the Primus. The boy glanced around the room with keen interest and expressed his admiration for the keeper's way of life, enthusing about the "rustic simplicity", the unsophisticated cooking apparatus, the water cistern, and most of all the view from the window.

While the tea steeped in a pot on the table, the visitor asked if he might use Ethan's "washroom".

"You can wash up at the kitchen sink," said Ethan.

"Um, I mean the toilet."

"Ah. Well, it's a wooden outhouse at the end of the work shed. I hope you don't mind its rustic simplicity."

"No, not at all. It adds to the atmosphere."

"It surely does," said Ethan.

After drinking good strong cups of tea, the near-black tannic acid tempered by condensed milk, they went out for a tour of the vacated nest holes.

The boy was a talker. Undeterred by Ethan's minimal responses, he described his several encounters with their favorite bird, what he knew about its curious quirks and charms. Ethan contributed his own observations. But there was only so much one could discuss about puffins, and

93

before long he began to wonder when the visitor would depart.

When they ran out of things to say, the boy gazed about the island with a whimsical look and said, "I guess everyone dreams of being a lighthouse keeper at one time or other."

"Oh, not everyone," Ethan demurred.

"I sure do. Or I did. I'm finishing up my degree this coming year, then it's down to the sea in ships, as the saying goes." A smile. "How did you ever get to be keeper here?"

"A coincidence."

"A *coincidence*? Didn't you apply to the Coast Guard and take courses?"

"I suppose that's the way it's done now, but when I was younger, things were a bit more casual."

"When did you first move out here?"

"Oh, about twenty years ago."

"You must have been a child."

"I was eighteen years old or thereabouts."

"Really? You look way younger. So, how did you get here?"

"I was walking the coast of Cape Breton one summer. I'd just finished my second year of logging over on the mainland—cutting timber and skidding logs to the bush roads. One place I worked, they still used horses."

"Are you saying you were *sixteen* when you started logging?"

"Yes. I was strong then."

"You look pretty strong now. So, what came next?"

"I wasn't sure what to do with my life—just hiking around, waiting for the future to happen. This one morning, I was eating breakfast in a café in Glace Bay, when I overheard two men in uniform at the next table,

94

talking about the lighthouse at Brendan's Harbour needing help. The keeper was old and not doing so well, they said. I went over to their table and asked how I could sign up."

"Huh. And just like that, you were signed up?"

"Well, no, they told me I was too young and I'd need training. But I offered to volunteer, maybe help out for the summer. I had some money saved, and I wouldn't need payment, just wanted to try it out for the experience. They gave me a phone number to call. I guess the authorities were desperate enough to take me on."

How old was he now? Thirty-seven? No, thirty-eight, last time he had thought about it. There were documents he could check, but it didn't matter. He lived. He swam in the waters of time, pulled along by its currents.

"And how old are you?" Ethan asked, to avoid abruptness, or the gruffness he sometimes suspected in himself—and to move the conversation to a round conclusion, hastening the lad on his way.

"I turned twenty this past March," said the boy. "It was almost April Fools' Day. Beat it by a couple of hours."

As they trekked back to the tower, and presumably toward departure from the cove, the visitor said:

"By the way, I don't see any boats here. How do you get in and out?"

"There's a causeway. I can walk it now and then." Ethan pointed west to the place where the sands sometimes appeared.

"Sounds kind of cut off," said the visitor.

"Not really. I've been working on a boat."

"Can I see it?" said the boy with childish eagerness.

Doing a quick mental check, Ethan concluded that this would be harmless enough, as his wooden family was safely stowed out of sight in the big sea locker.

"All right," he said.

Ethan opened up the shed doors, and the *Puffin* materialized like an apparition, dazzling white in the shafts of sunlight that broke into the shadowy interior.

"Oh, she's a beauty!" the boy exclaimed, walking slowly all around her.

He grinned at the name on the stern, and peered closely at the figurehead.

"Perfect!" he said. "Did you build the boat from scratch?"

"A wreck," said Ethan. "Pulled her up from the rocks. I'm rebuilding her."

"She looks totally rebuilt to me, in fact ready to launch."

"That would be quite a chore," said Ethan, shaking his head.

He mumbled a few reasons why the boat was not ready, but even as he spoke he knew they were unconvincing.

"I could help you launch her," said the visitor.

"Oh, no, it would take time ... and ..."

"I've got time."

Ethan said nothing, gazed at his boots, deliberated.

While he was mulling it over, the boy said, "I see you've got block and tackle, and plenty of rope. A few logs for rollers. Two men could do it."

"I could pay you for your help," Ethan said at last, looking up.

"I don't need any payment, just want to try it out for the experience. The way you did, all those years ago."

"Well, I don't know ..."

"I wouldn't be any trouble. You wouldn't have to lodge me, since I've got my gear and tent. Hey, if you let me stay, I'll pay *you*!"

"No, no, you won't pay me."

Realizing that he had been outmaneuvered by the boy, and also thinking that the time had indeed come to launch the boat, he said, "All right."

So Ross hauled his gear up from the shore and pitched a synthetic dome tent beside the tower. It was late afternoon by then, the day too far gone to start the launching process, which Ethan estimated would take two or three days. He made a fish chowder for their supper, locally called "hugger-in-buff": fresh cod chunks, chopped bacon bits, diced potatoes and onions, all simmering in a sauce made from four cans of cream of mushroom soup. They ate at the kitchen table, Ethan tipping his bowl up and draining its contents into his mouth as his visitor watched with a humorous look and consumed his own portion with a spoon. They finished up with some stale maple leaf cookies and a pot of tea, trading morsels of hardware knowledge and seabird lore until Ross yawned, said an early good-night, and went out to his tent to sleep.

The weather the next morning was auspicious—warm with a light breeze and the sky a wide cerulean blue, with thin clouds feathering high above.

Years before, Ethan had worked out the engineering for winching the *Puffin* down to the cove. Eyebolts strategically placed around the boat's belly, just below the gunwales, enabled the looping of hemp cables, which in turn were fed through block and tackle, and a crank winch at the stern. Safety ropes were secured to the shed's upright beams with their own smaller winches, which could be loosened as the boat descended.

Working side by side, Ethan and the boy laid out a corduroy road of twelve logs in front of the bow, the top of each coated with yellow petroleum grease, positioning them in such a way that they equaled the entire length of the boat and extended beyond her several feet to support the keel as she inched forward.

The ground was level in the shed, so gravity was no help at this first stage. Thus, a second set of ropes, pulleys, and winches was needed, secured to an iron bar that Ethan pounded by sledgehammer into the turf about twenty feet off the bow. Once the boat was out of the shed and the ground began to slope downward, the boat's weight would then assist her descent.

It took the better part of the morning to set it all up. They broke for a quick lunch, and then they went back to work, eager to get going again. The front winch operated just fine, slowly drawing the boat out onto the logs and into the sunlight, not without a few creaks and the constant sound of soft scraping as the keel slipped over the rollers. With Ethan maintaining the winch's hand crank, Ross took it upon himself to remove a log from the rear and carry it around to the front, extending the path ahead. Again and again he repeated this as the boat moved forward. Two hours later, they had her close to a steeper incline.

Ethan kicked a wood block under the bow to secure it while he undid the frontward ropes and winch. After that, he hammered sideways on the iron bar until it was loose, and then pulled it out of the turf. Now all the boat's weight was on the restraining ropes and the winch in the shed. When he kicked the blocks out of the bow, the ropes tightened and gently groaned as gravity took over. Ross reverse-winched, giving the ropes slack, letting the boat slide forward little by little. It was Ethan's turn to carry logs from the track they had covered and lay them down in front of the bow, making the pathway as he went. By nightfall, the boat was more than halfway to the cove. There had been no mishaps, and they were pleased with the progress. By mutual agreement, they called it a day.

The next morning, Ethan fried buckwheat pancakes and an omelet made from powdered eggs and canned bacon. Then, ready to begin the next stage, he and Ross topped themselves off from the coffee pot and went outside to resume the tasks they had left off the day before. The weather was again fine, almost no wind, with long, slow ocean swells heaving in from the east. Little was said between the man and boy, and it was pleasurable for both to experience the intuitive coordination of tasks. No instructions were needed. Ross seemed to know exactly what to do, and when to do it. The constant cranking of the winch handle was a strain on the arm, however, so they spelled each other every half hour. By noon the *Puffin*'s bow was perched over the rim of the sharper grade leading down to the sandy cove.

It was too nice a day to eat inside, so Ethan went back to the cottage and filled a thermos with coffee. He slathered leftover pancakes with jam, stacked them on a tin plate, and brought the feast back to Ross. The boy was lying on the grass with his hands behind his head, eyes closed, soaking up the sun.

Ethan stood a moment, regarding the visitor, noting to himself that from the beginning he had called him *the boy*, and it had developed into a habit. In truth he was a young man, and a very strong young man at that. But he looked younger than his years, and *boy* was a serviceable word, one less syllable, two less than *visitor*, easier on the mind.

"Lunch," said Ethan.

The boy's eyes sprang open, and he jumped to his feet with incredible energy. He strode back to his tent, returning a minute later with a bag of hiker's trail mix and two oranges.

They sat down in the shade of the boat.

"This is great," Ross said. "This is one of the most marvelous days I've ever experienced. I'll remember it all my life."

"All your life?" said Ethan, accepting an orange, which he peeled a little too eagerly. Biting into it he tasted the deluge of citric sweetness, like bliss on the tongue, for he did not get much fruit in his life. It was gone in seconds. Watching this, Ross tried to force the other one upon him. Ethan at first declined, arguing for equal shares, but his resistance in the matter was thin. He ate the second orange with such gusto that Ross began to laugh.

"Vitamin C," Ross said. "Looks like you're starved for it."

"Oh well, I get some of it once a year. The wild roses down by the cove."

"I didn't notice any roses."

"There's bushes of them, but the flowers are past blooming now; they're turning into rose hips. When they ripen, they'll be as big as a grape. I eat a shipload of them in August, early September, every year."

"Maybe you should dry some, eat them in winter."

Ethan pondered this, absentmindedly chewing on a piece of orange peel, then swallowing it.

"That's a good idea," he said, nodding. "I'll try it."

"Um, Ethan," said Ross, looking perplexed, "when we get the *Puffin* down to the water, what are you going to tether her with?"

"Tether her?"

"You know, like, tie her up to a wharf or a buoy. I don't see anything on her that looks permanent. I mean, there's no bow ring."

Ruefully, Ethan chuckled.

"Something funny?" asked the boy with a smile.

"Well, yes, kind of. I spent ten years on this boat and never once thought about a bow ring."

"Never? That's amazing, considering you're surrounded by boats, all of them with bow rings." He paused, musing. "Maybe the *Puffin* was something mystical in your mind."

"Mystical?"

"Like a dream you were in love with. And now the dream's finally ready to launch, needing a couple of details you hadn't thought about when she was just floating around in your mind."

"Maybe. Yes, you could be right."

"So, d'you want me to nip into the harbor and pick one up? I'll take my boat and be back in an hour or two."

"If you would, please. I'll drill the hole while you're gone."

"Okay, and I'll bring some guards too."

"Guards?"

"You know, fenders to protect the gunwales and hull when you're docking. Even a wooden dock can batter a boat badly."

Ethan was now thoroughly embarrassed, and a little mystified by himself.

All these years, he thought as he forced some cash into Ross's hands.

"And anything else you can think of," he shouted as the boy fired up his motor.

Suddenly aware of his brain's rather disturbing selectivity, which had just been pointed out to him, he could not make sense of how he had overlooked such important details. Then he wondered if maybe life itself was like that: you focused on one big thing and missed the small things that could prove to be just as essential. At other times you focused on small things and missed the big ones.

With a brace and bit he drilled the hole beneath the feet of the puffin figurehead. He widened the hole with successively larger bits. The beam was aged hardwood, and it was tough work getting through it, but this was good, for it would be durable. He had just finished the job when he heard the rumble of Ross's boat returning.

Excited and glowing with pride of accomplishment, the boy trudged up the slope from the cove, weighed down with loops of chain over his shoulders and a bag of hardware in hand.

"Got it all, Ethan. Plus thirty feet of chain for the anchor line. The guards are in my boat; I'll bring 'em up later. I got twelve nylon-reinforced fenders, six per side, toggled for hanging over the side or for storing inboard."

"Did I give you enough money?"

"Don't worry about it," he laughed. "I kept the change."

It was a joke, and it looked to Ethan that the boy had paid from his own pocket.

"Give me the total," he insisted.

"Mmm, I forget."

"Then I'll need to see the receipts."

"Lost them," said Ross with a grin, and Ethan gave up.

"Thanks," he said as the boy handed him a steel ring with threaded couplers at the open ends of it. And then, less perfunctory, "Thank you, Ross."

It was the first time he had used Ross's name, and the boy's eyes flashed an acknowledgment.

By the end of the day, they had winched the *Puffin* down onto the sand, close to the granite quay. The beach was flatter than the ground immediately above it but still sloped enough to permit some forward movement. Beyond this point, however, gravity would be of little help. The sun was lowering in the west as they set blocks under the bow and alongside the keel. As an additional precaution, Ethan roped the bow ring to the iron spike on the quay.

That evening, Ross begged permission to accompany Ethan to the tower and keep watch with him through the night.

"An experience," he emphasized.

So Ethan gave him the grand tour.

Arriving at the watch room, the boy went up the ladder through the hatch to the catwalk, and scrambled around it, excited and flushed.

"Wow, that's some flashlight," he said, peering through the glass into the lantern room.

"The beacon has a Fresnel lens," said Ethan. "The highest order in the series, with maximum refraction for focusing the beam."

"I can't wait to see it going at night."

"If you looked into that beam, Ross, you'd be blinded for life."

The boy's chief interest was the watch room itself. He was fascinated by everything, had an inexhaustible supply of questions. Ethan described the clockwork's intricacies, unfolded a few maps of local waters, showed him the operation of the VHF and shortwave radios, and set him up with the telescope, where he could peer more closely at passing homebound trawlers and the lights of larger ships winking in the dusk, far out on the horizon.

The whole western sky was awash with crimson bleeding into emerald green.

"Red sky at night, sailors' delight," declared Ross. "Red sky at morning, sailors take warning."

"Not exactly science," said Ethan with a show of humor.

"But good poetry."

"And true, more often than not."

Ethan set the generator going in the shed and switched on the beacon. Ross enjoyed the spectacle for a few hours, but he had worked hard all day, and by midnight he was yawning frequently and had trouble keeping his eyes open. Ethan sent him down to the tent for a well-earned sleep. He dozed in his chair, rousing from time to time to check that the beacon was sweeping as regular as always. When the east turned silver with approaching dawn, he went down to the cottage and set the coffee brewing.

In his notebook he wrote:

—A momentous event today. The *Puffin* will be launched at last. A young fellow is helping me.
—I wonder if, after all these years in the making, she'll simply roll over and sink. Roll or sink or float, it doesn't half matter. For me, she's more a work of art than anything. But I can't deny that to see her float would be the greatest thrill of my life.
—Tired. A happy tired—a good feeling.
—Silvery harp seals sporting off the south end of the island. Haven't seen any for months. There must be something under the water there. The striped bass have been moving northward from the Carolinas the past few years, taking over our spawning rivers, eating up our indigenous fish—most worrisome, young salmon. I hope the seals are hunting bass, though maybe they're just playing.
—Clear sky. Weather the best.

After breakfast, Ethan and Ross carried two long pike poles down to the cove. First they laid the greased logs from the bow to the water's edge, and then they positioned themselves at the boat's stern. After inserting the ends of the pikes as far as possible on either side of the keel, they levered the poles with all their might, putting their shoulders to it and straining every muscle. The boat moved forward a little on the skids, but not by much. Again they tried, and again there was some progress.

Now the puffin figurehead was hovering above the lapping waves, though the base of the curved bow beam still sat on the logs. They paused to catch their breath, and then resumed their labors. It was exhausting, slow work, but inch by inch the boat moved forward.

"Down to the sea!" exclaimed Ross with a laugh, pausing to wipe the sweat from his brow.

"This is doing it the hard way," said Ethan. "Let's winch her."

It took some time to set up a winch, with a rope linking the iron bar on the quay to the boat's bow ring. The delay was well worth it, for now the labor was merely a case of repeated cranking. Half an hour later the boat was off the logs, with her nose lifted and the stern wet, though still scraping sand. Ross took over the cranking, and Ethan pushed from behind. Then came a soft skidding sound and the *Puffin* slid forward and rose, her weight fully borne by the water.

Ethan and Ross sat down on the quay and just looked at her, both of them smiling.

"Sailor's delight," mused the boy.

Ethan nodded, feeling a good deal more than delight, in fact glowing with an exultation that he had never experienced before. There she was, riding where she was meant to be, a thing damaged and restored, more beautiful than she had ever been. She was poised and evenly balanced, rising and falling with the gentle surf.

Ross unbuckled the winch and pulled on the rope, swinging the bow in an arc that brought her nose pointing to the quay. When it was near enough he jumped onto the bow plate, scrambled over the cabin roof, and dropped into the midsection. There, he flipped the fenders on their toggles, letting them fall over the gunwales. That done, he stood with arms akimbo and legs spread wide, deliberately making the boat rock from side to side.

"Come aboard, captain!" he called with a grin.

So Ethan did. He sat down on the plank seat at midship, and simply marveled. No more was said for a time.

There came a moment when Ross frowned with a puzzled look.

"Um, Ethan, I see the oarlocks here, but I don't see any oars. No motor either."

"I've got a motor on order. It's been on order for more than a year. I'm paying for it bit by bit."

"That doesn't sound quite right. Aren't you supposed to get the motor first and pay it off gradually?"

"I'm not sure. I've never been much good with figures."

"Nor the ways of the big bad world, is my guess. How about we take my boat to the harbor and look around, check out other options?"

After tying up at the main dock in Brendan's Harbour, Ethan went searching for any local fishermen who were not out on the water. He found a few men pottering about their boats, and all of them told him the same thing: there weren't any good used motors to be had, leastways not that they knew about; the only possibility was at the chandler's shop.

"He's sellin' new mostly, but he's got a few clunkers out back, if you want to check them over," said one. "Hold tight to yer wallet," said another.

The chandler, Mr. Biggs, greeted Ethan in a friendly manner, and eyed Ross without comment.

Ethan told the man he had heard he had some used motors for sale, and would like to look at them.

"Well, sure," said Biggs, "though you're maybe forgettin' the deposit on the Evinrude."

"Haven't forgotten," said Ethan. "I'd just like to see the older items. It can't hurt to have two motors."

"As a kinda backup, like," chuckled the chandler. "Very wise."

Biggs went out through a door at the rear of the shop, beckoning that Ethan should follow.

"This is ridiculous," muttered Ross, checking price tags on half a dozen outboard motors. "Sixteen to eighteen thousand dollars, plus tax. And this one's for twenty thousand. I could buy a new car for that. How long before you've paid it in full—decades?"

"I haven't thought too much about it, since I wasn't sure when the *Puffin* would be launched. Figured I'd lay down a larger sum when the time came."

"A used one makes more sense, costs a lot less money. No warranty, of course, but if it's solid and doesn't quit on you—"

"Come on back here!" shouted Biggs.

The room they now entered was a small warehouse filled with marine equipment. Three battered outboard motors were clamped to sawhorses by an open double door leading to a yard full of small wrecked boats and a larger fishing vessel on a timber cradle.

Ethan made straightway to an old Johnson 90 hp. He felt he knew the motor from somewhere, and then with a jolt of recognition he realized it was the very motor that had been only a turn of a screw from pulling Esau to the bottom of the sea. No doubt the hood had been hand painted by Esau himself, slapdash purple with orange symbolic flames.

"That's Esau Hurley's motor," he said to the chandler.

The man shrugged. "Yep, I'm selling off his stuff to cover his debts. He owed me plenty."

"I'll need to fire it up," Ethan said to the chandler.

"No need to run it," the man replied. "It's as good as new."

"Still, I want to hear the motor."

"I'll give you a minute."

"I need ten or fifteen."

The chandler gave Ethan an aggrieved look.

"D'you really need to hear it run for ten minutes? Ain't my word good enough for you?"

"I just like to know what I'm buying," said Ethan, without letting himself be pushed into backing down.

Looking disgusted, Biggs hooked up a water hose to an attachment that he clipped onto the stem of the outboard, and turned a tap.

"What is that?" Ethan asked.

"Water cooler. You dry-run this Cadillac, and you'll burn it out."

Biggs attached a jerry can and fuel line to the motor. When he pulled the rip cord the engine sputtered once or twice, blew a single gust of exhaust, and then steadied. It hummed nicely for several minutes without a skip.

As Ethan listened, his head cocked at an angle, the better to catch any imperfections, he asked himself whether buying Esau's motor would make him prey to unhappy memories, would be a constant source of sadness. In the end, he thought not, telling himself that having this motor would be a reminder of the importance—and the consequences—of rescues. A life saved in exchange for a few hours lost and a bad case of bronchitis. A good trade. Of course, he would paint over its lurid colors with something more sedate.

"Purrs like a kitten," said the chandler.

"I'll take it," Ethan said with a nod.

"Well, you've got twelve hundred dollars on deposit. We can call it square."

"I'll give you four hundred dollars for the motor."

Biggs gave his suspenders a nasty snap.

"What! You're not a thief, are you, McQuarry? Listen, I'll throw in the gas can and lines, and we can call it even."

"Doesn't sound even to me," Ross interjected. "That makes eight hundred dollars for a gas can."

"Who are you?" asked the chandler with a dead tone and ice in his eyes.

"The hired help. My boss here isn't so good with sums. I'm the negotiator."

Ethan was wryly amused by the boy's intervention, a relative stranger treating him as if he were slow-witted and needed minding.

"The negotiator, are you?" said the chandler. "Well, why don't you negotiate yourself right out of my business."

"Sure, happy to go. I was just on my way to discuss your business practices with the folks at the dock and the other places I'll be going today, which is pretty much everywhere. Not to mention the article I'll be writing for the newspaper in Glace Bay."

Thoroughly rankled, Biggs thrust his jaw forward as his face reddened.

"You little—"

"Ross," said Ethan. "Thanks, I can handle the transaction myself. Why don't you wait for me outside."

For the moment, Ross chose to ignore him, leaning closer to the chandler with a grim expression.

"What you said about Ethan is true," he said. "He's no thief. I hope that applies to somebody else here."

The chandler's fists clenched tight, and his chest inflated to threat level.

"Ross, please," said Ethan.

"I'll be waiting outside," said the boy with a hard look at Biggs.

When he was gone, Ethan said mildly, "I'll take the offer, if you throw in *two* new fuel tanks and hoses. I'll also be needing a few other things. Long oars, an anchor. Including the outboard, it wouldn't amount to more than a thousand dollars all told. You'd be making a profit of two hundred. And wiping out Esau Hurley's debt to you as well. What do you say?"

Snap, snap, snap with a scowl for emphasis.

"Skillsaw Hurley's debt is a different matter," said Biggs.

"Mmm," said Ethan. "But it's a debt beyond repayment. At least not payable by him. I'd be glad to contribute in his stead."

After a little more dickering, a satisfactory agreement was reached, just as Ethan had proposed it. When all the business was concluded, with legal receipts signed, he called Ross back into the shop. Together, they gathered the items Ethan had managed to obtain in the exchange and carried them down the street to Ross's boat. Then back they went to the chandlery, where they unclamped the motor from the sawhorse and carried it away.

"You were robbed, Ethan," the boy muttered.

"Oh well, maybe so. Or maybe not."

Which drew a puzzled look from the boy.

Despite the single sour note on the morning's proceedings, it was otherwise a most beautiful day. Back on the island Ross helped Ethan stow his purchases aboard the *Puffin* and clamp the motor to her stern. Using a rust-resistant lacquer paint, Ethan spent an hour covering the garish flames and the purple casing with a Lincoln green, which made a good visual combination with the boat's red trim. Under the ministrations of the sun and warm breeze, it was dry to the touch by suppertime.

After their evening meal, they fired up Esau's motor and took the *Puffin* out of the cove, making way at a leisurely pace. Ross stood by the cabin, his arms folded on its roof, chin on his arms, gazing ahead beyond the bow. Ethan at the throttle guided her around the island and headed north in the direction of Wreck Isle. His face looked suitably solemn for the occasion, but inside himself he was wild with elation. He did not push the boat, just let her coast along, comfortably taking the waves. As stout as a real puffin, she nevertheless moved through the water like a spear, clean and true. The motor did not fail.

With the tide near its height, Wreck Isle was presently invisible, barely submerged, a hazard if one did not know the waters. Ethan slowed the boat as he carefully circled the rock, and then he headed back toward home. Though he and Ross were longing for more time with the *Puffin*, night was coming on. They brought her carefully into the cove as darkness fell.

In the morning Ross said, "I've gotta be on my way, Ethan. My boat's a rental, and I have to have it back in Sydney by tonight."

Ethan observed the rosy mist lifting off the relatively calm water.

"A long voyage," he said, "but you should make it with time to spare."

Together they collapsed the tent and packed it up. Ethan helped carry the gear down to Ross's boat.

"Well, good luck," he said as they stood on the beach, shaking hands.

"It was great to meet you, Ethan."

"Thank you for your help, Ross."

"If I'm ever back this way ...," the boy prompted.

"If you do come this way again, please drop in."

"I will. Take care, Ethan."

"Take care."

"Keep the light burning."

They said no more. Ethan stood on the quay, watching as the boat drew away and returning Ross's final wave of the hand. He was still watching as the boat disappeared into the mist. Then, without moving, he looked long at the *Puffin* rising and falling on the diminishing wake, loving her, very glad for her launching, and grateful, too, for the unexpected visitor. He shook his head, remembering that only a few days ago he had wondered if the boat would ever be launched. And now here she was—bobbing up and down, as pretty as a picture. Life's latest surprise.

The return to solitude was a relief in a way. It was back to normal routine, normal silences, and the opportunity to stand by the edge of the island without fear of interruption, gazing out to sea, listening to the listeningness, sensing the awakeness of things. Even so, he felt a new kind of absence, and he now realized that the visitor had been of benefit to him in more than the boat's launching. This first experience of companionship, he understood by hindsight, had not been in the words exchanged but in the presence.

In late August he gathered sacks of rose hips, eating almost as much as he saved, drying the remainder on the grass during hot shining days. The birds made off with a few, but Ethan thought that was all right. The wild fruit was plentiful, and when its season was over, he was pleased to see that he had accumulated enough to feed himself a few per day during the coming winter.

In the same month, a miniature guest arrived on the island, a ruby-throated hummingbird that buzzed his red checkered bush shirt while he was sitting on the grass with his back leaning against the tower, dozing and baking himself in the sun. It flew backward and forward with astonishing aerobatics, trying to assess whether he was a giant flower. It landed for a moment on the top of his knee and then fled in the direction of the mainland.

There was also the morning when he stepped off his porch into a low-lying cloud that hovered above the grass, the cloud's colors changing from deep blue to maroon as the breeze played with it. It was a swarm of butterflies such as he had never seen before—coming from somewhere, going somewhere else, resting a while on his island.

And not long after, while beachcombing on the causeway, barefoot and wearing only shorts, the burning sun on his back, he walked bent over, entranced as always by the variety of smaller seashells washed up after storms. On this day, however, he came upon a shell more exotic than any he had yet collected. It was shaped like a fat tuba, mauve with a pink interior, rimmed with tiny portholes, as if designed by a creative engineer. Nearby he found a white sand dollar the size of his palm. Embossed on its circular form was a five-leafed design surrounded by symmetrical decorative beads, the work of a perfectionist jeweler.

He savored each of these phenomena as if they were benevolences of a mysterious generosity in nature. Smiling over each one with a look of childlike glee— which would have surprised him if he could have observed himself—he whispered, *Thank you, thank you, thank you,* not knowing to whom he spoke. Later, during the night watch, he wrote descriptions of his findings—rose hips, hummingbird, butterflies, tuba, and sand dollar—in his notebook.

The waning of summer stretched longer that year, melting seamlessly into an unusually benign autumn, the sun shining day after day. And though the moon dragged the bulk of the ocean this way and that, and the wind sometimes blew hard, there were no serious storms. Taking advantage of the mild weather, Ethan navigated the *Puffin* into Brendan's Harbour at least once a week, enjoying at last the consequence of years of labor. As old as the motor was, it did not once fail him and was proving to be more powerful than he had anticipated. He took dedicated care of it, dismantled and reassembled parts, greased and oiled whatever needed it, and he kept the fuel line scrupulously clean. Only a needle and the float valve in the carburetor needed replacing. He also spent hours in discussion with boatmen at the wharf, gaining knowledge of how to protect the motor from deteriorating. One of them told him that Esau Hurley had fussed over the thing as if it were his own baby.

Ethan took the *Puffin* farther out on the Atlantic, testing speeds, testing the way she behaved in different kinds of waves and swells and winds. And there he learned that not only was she as stout and brave as her namesake, but she was dependable. Once he went up the coast to Glace Bay and brought back a cargo of groceries for better meals. There was heavy chop on the way home, and sudden squalls escalating to eighteen and twenty knots, but the boat rode through it well. There were no leaks.

On one of his excursions to Brendan's Harbour, he plundered the hardware store, buying new files for his wood chisels, new workmen's clothes, better rubber boots, and an electric barber's razor to improve his disgraceful appearance. After that, he gathered the mail, went to the library (there were no fines to pay), and finally stopped in at Elsie's place to bring her a little gift.

"Tea, Ethan?" she asked as he shook off his sea boots at the door.

"Please," he said, worried, as always, that he was intruding.

"Did you walk in?"

"No, I have a boat now."

"*Puffin*, you call her."

"You heard?"

"Nothing stays long unheard in a place as small as this," she said with an amused beam in her eyes.

"I suppose that's true," he said ruefully. "I wanted to tell you myself."

Failing to know why he felt so disappointed, he thought about it a little. He concluded that something inside him had wanted to reassure her personally, for her maternal anxiety had more than once urged him to get a proper boat. She had worried about him, and to have someone worry about him was a rare thing—in fact, a wonderful thing.

"I could show her to you, if you'd like. Take you for a ride too."

"I'd love to see her, Ethan. But as for rides, dear, I can't swim, and I've always been wary of water, prone to seasickness too, which is a sorry thing to say of a shorebird like me."

"Someone has to stay ashore to welcome sailors home."

It was out of his mouth before he recalled that her husband had never made it home.

"Mmm," she said, nodding, apparently making no connection.

"Now, I just finished making a crowberry pie," she said. "Crowberry tastes like mealy mash, so I added lots of sugar.

A few wild strawberries and my own rhubarb chopped up fine should give it a zing. Can I test it on you?"

"I'm willing."

"You might die."

"I'll risk it."

So he went into the visitor's parlor crowded with tables and chairs, noting that he was the only customer.

Half a pie and a pot of tea later, he bent over a bag he had carried in and had left on the floor, half-hidden by his legs. From it he removed one of his little carvings. A fishing boat.

When Elsie came by to clean off the dishes, he said, "This is for you. Thought you might like it."

"Oh my!" she breathed, her face growing serious as she stepped forward to receive it into her hands, forgetting to wipe them on her apron. "This is amazing. Where did you get such a fine thing?"

"I made it."

"No!"

"I did."

She turned it around and around, inspecting the details.

"Oh, that's clever, those beads for lights, and the rigging just right. And the crane and nets! And look at the cabin; is that real glass in the windows? And such pretty colors for the hull and trim."

When she came to the stern and saw the name of the boat, she fell silent, and her eyes filled with tears.

"How did you know?" she asked.

"Well, I, um . . . ," he murmured.

She bent over and kissed him on the top of his head, and quickly left the room for her kitchen.

He had wanted to say, *It's for your husband, for you to remember him by. So that his boat is not matchsticks, that he is not lost forever at the bottom of the sea, that he's with you still.*

But realized in time that this would be a foolish overabundance of explanation, and that she understood everything.

No one had kissed him in decades, not even on the top of his head. He was still discombobulated when she came back into the visitor's parlor and sat down across the table from him.

"Thank you," she said.

"You're welcome."

She poured him another cup of tea. She put milk into it, the way he liked it. He didn't get much milk out there on the island.

"There's an ocean inside," she said at last. And paused. "Inside everyone."

He nodded and nodded.

"And sometimes people drown in it."

He wasn't sure what she meant, and could produce no reply.

She stood abruptly and carried the boat to a high shelf facing the entrance. After shifting a few decorative plates and a purple starfish, she put the boat in pride of place. With no more said, she wrapped up the remaining pie and sent him away with it.

Throughout the following week he replayed her comment often.

There's an ocean inside, she had said. *Inside everyone. And sometimes people drown in it.*

What had she meant? Was it, "There's an ocean inside you, Ethan, and other people drown in its depths"? Or was it, "There's an ocean inside everyone, and sometimes they drown in their own depths"? Or had she meant that she, herself, had been sinking into the abyss of her loss, and his gift had rescued her?

Perhaps she had meant none of these—or all of them at once.

On his next visit to town, he dropped by the chandlery and bought a vinyl cover for the motor, and a canvas canopy for the open part of the boat, along with the snaps and hooks it needed. Biggs was congenial enough, though he tossed in a pithy epithet about "that kid", the one Ethan had brought into the shop a few months back, and said he sure hoped he had fired the "loudmouth".

"Well, I don't expect I'll see him again," said Ethan, noting that Biggs was the sort of man who kept a tight grip on his resentments. Which was something worth knowing.

Back home, he cut a flap in the canopy near the stern, sewing up the seams with a sail needle and tough thread. Then he installed snaps to keep it closed tight. This innovation was a precaution, for a time when he might need to sit at the stern as he brought the boat through bad weather, for there was no wheel in the cabin and no rudder. Of course, he would avoid such situations, but one never knew.

As autumn retreated under the advance of what looked to become a miserable winter, Ethan tethered the *Puffin* to a buoy chained by cement blocks dropped into two fathoms of water, a few yards out from the beach, close by the causeway. There she would be safe from strong currents and winds, bobbing about and waiting for spring.

With no one to invade his privacy, he began work on a four-foot-long model boat, copying a design he had found in a book on eighteenth-century fishing vessels. The hull was a single piece of log that he cut and planed to perfect symmetry; its smaller parts he hand whittled from scraps of lumber or crafted from metal and thread and canvas. In early December he painted her brightly—a sea-green hull, red cabin and trimmings, unbleached linen sails. A little man at the wheel. A rudder that swiveled. Anchors and lights and brasswork. When she was done to his satisfaction, with her ancient name painted on the stern, he carried her out to the *Puffin* at ebb tide, up to his thighs in hip waders, shivering and happy.

On his last voyage of the season, he docked at the wharf in Brendan's Harbour, noting the Christmas decorations on the storefronts, and merry lights in many home windows. Dark was falling as he carried the model boat, hidden in black plastic bags, up the town slope to the new church. He left it by the front door, and walked swiftly away.

The Return

Winter that year was not unkind to the *Puffin*. There were a few wild storms that gave Ethan anxiety, but she rode through them with admirable ease. In mid-March he brought the motor out of storage in the work shed, pulled the boat to the quay, and got everything shipshape for her second season.

Being mobile again took some getting used to. It seemed a great luxury, a lavishness of riches. Going back and forth to the harbor, pretty much whenever he wanted, was changing his consciousness, he knew. It meant less solitude, of course, but this was acceptable because he was still in control of whom he saw and for how long. Moreover, he was eating a good deal more fresh food than he had throughout his life. He felt healthier all told, and eager for the summer.

He did wonder if the warmer weather would bring a repeat of the previous summer's uncanny influx of visitors. He hoped not, and yet on the other hand he wondered if Catherine MacInnis would come hiking this way again. If she did, this time he would invite her to stay awhile. He would make a very good meal for her. He would take her out on the ocean for a ride, show her the boat released into the elements like a freed bird, doing what a boat should do. She might kiss the figurehead again. She might even, if things went well, kiss its maker. And he would not neglect to ask for her mailing address, so that he could write to her when she was gone—to speak of his deepest thoughts and his feelings for her.

Paying little attention to the passage of time, by the end of the month he was still chiseling away at a new creation in the kitchen. Near completion, it was a boy riding the back of an arching dolphin, about three feet long. Visitors, if any, would not yet arrive for weeks. The season was squally, the rain off and on for days, the brief respites of clear weather allowing only a pale disk of sun to appear through mist and fog. He still had plenty of time to move his secret creations out to the sea locker in the work shed.

One afternoon, rising from a nap, he heard the rumble of a high-power motor nearby. He dressed with his usual indifference to appearance, sure that the boat was passing the island, close off his shore. But when the motor was killed abruptly, he went outside to see if there was an intrusion in the offing. Still half asleep, he stepped off the porch and ambled downslope toward the cove. A young man was walking up over the crest.

It was Ross Campbell.

"Ethan!" the boy called, waving.

A few steps later and they were shaking hands. Ethan was not unhappy to see him, but, as always, he was concerned about the break in his solitude.

"I see the *Puffin*'s looking great," said the boy.

"Yes, she made it through winter without any problems. I used her a lot last fall, after you left. The past few weeks I've been taking her into the harbor again."

"Well, I've got a boat of my own now too. I'm dying to show you. Drove her up from Halifax, parked the trailer at the wharf in the harbor."

"Are you making another tour of the coast?"

"That's the plan. But I thought I'd drop in to see how you are."

"I'm fine," said Ethan. He paused, searching for something to say. "The puffins are nesting here now. I could show you."

"I'd love to see them."

"You'll have to be quiet."

"I can be quiet."

Ethan went into the cottage to get his binoculars, and then together he and Ross trod softly through the grass beyond the tower. They dropped to their knees and began to crawl toward the rocky bluff facing the open ocean. Soon the line of nests appeared in the grass, and the low growling of puffin talk reached them on the light breeze.

"Sounds like a flock of baaing sheep," whispered Ross.

"Tiny chainsaws," Ethan whispered back, and the boy clamped a hand over his mouth to suppress a laugh.

Exchanging the binoculars back and forth, they watched the birds' comings and goings for a while, the diving and fishing and feeding. If the puffins detected the human presence, they gave no sign of it.

After a time they inched their way backward and returned to the cottage.

Standing by the kitchen door, Ethan hemmed and hawed, worrying about the dolphin. In the end, he decided that no harm would come from letting Ross see it, and invited him in.

As Ethan put the kettle on to boil, Ross sat down at the table and spotted the carving.

"Whoa, what's this?" he exclaimed, his head jerking back in astonishment.

"It's just something I'm making."

"It's more than *something*, Ethan. This is fantastic. It's, well, it's really beautiful."

The boy's words were said without his usual ebullience. It was as if he were whispering to puffins. And Ethan was the puffin.

"I should have guessed," said Ross. "I mean, you carved the figurehead for the boat. It makes sense you'd be pouring out other masterpieces."

"Masterpieces," echoed Ethan with a doubtful smile.

"This is really ... elegant."

After Ethan had set the tea to steep in a pot, he rustled about the kitchen cupboards looking for fixings for lunch.

"I've got a can of corned beef. Is corned beef okay? There's some butter left too, on the verge of going rancid, so it would be best to eat it now. And biscuits I made a few days ago. Getting a bit hard, but I soften them up with molasses."

Ross grinned. "Oh yeah, that sounds ..."

"Elegant?"

They laughed.

As they ate, Ross told Ethan that he had brought a few things for him to look at. Not just his new boat but some odds and ends he had picked up in Halifax. They might be useful out here on the island.

After lunch they walked down to the cove, where Ethan was impressed by the shining new Lund, an eighteen footer with a big outboard on the stern.

"She cost a lot," said Ross, "but I received a grant for the summer research I'm doing."

"Marine biology," Ethan said.

"You remembered. That's right, marine biology— saltwater organisms, mainly. Birds are a personal interest."

Pulling back a canvas, he uncovered clear plastic bins full of scientific objects, the purpose of which Ethan could not guess.

"Here's what I wanted to show you," said Ross, pulling the canvas back farther. "I got this stuff at a bankruptcy sale, some kind of alternative energy warehouse. I waited out the last bids and bought it for next to nothing."

It appeared to be a turbine with four-foot blades and a small motor the size of a fist, with lengths of wire wrapped around it.

"Wind generator," explained Ross. "It was damaged, but I cleaned the coils, rewired, tinkered, replaced the bearings. It works fine now. It's yours if you want it. A gift, I mean."

Ethan considered the offer.

"Thank you for the thought, Ross, but I wouldn't know what to do with it. Or how to connect it."

"I can help you with that. And I've brought the twelve-volt batteries it needs. The generator recharges them once the wind starts blowing the propellers. Above eight or ten miles per hour, it produces a kilowatt per hour. You get a lot of wind out here, don't you?"

"Fairly constant. But I have the diesel generator."

"What if the generator fails someday or your fuel runs out? How long would the tower's backup batteries last?"

"Maybe twenty-four hours. But this little turbine couldn't power the beacon light and rotate it."

"True, but if your main system fails, the wind can keep your radio going and a few household lightbulbs too. Might come in handy someday."

"All right," said Ethan, chuckling. "You win."

"I knew I would. Can we start packing this stuff up to your place now?"

"Yes, let's. But this time I am paying you for it."

"No, you're not. You could compensate me by giving me room and board for a couple of days, like last year."

Ethan sighed inwardly, defeated but oddly pleased.

They unshipped Ross's gear and carried it up to the work shed, where it would be safe out of the elements for the duration of his visit. The boxes contained some delicate instruments, the boy explained, and he would prefer not to have it tossed about in his boat if a storm blew up. He had biological specimen containers and scuba diving equipment as well. The battery array for the wind generator came last—six 12-volt blocks clamped together into a square bank—so heavy that it was a two-man job getting it up to the work shed.

As Ross had done the previous year, he pitched his tent beside the tower entrance. Meanwhile, Ethan opened more tins and began putting together an evening meal sufficient for two. While a stew was cooking, he placed the dolphin on top of the unlighted heater, cleared the shavings off the table, and swept the floor. Soon there came a knock at the open door, with the boy leaning inside.

"No need to knock while you're staying here," said Ethan.

"Can I do anything to help with supper?"

"No, we're almost ready. Oh, there's a box of crackers there in the storage room, if you wouldn't mind getting it."

Ross opened the door to the pantry and went in. He was gone but a moment when he reemerged with a box of soda biscuits.

"Oh, wow!" he said, eyebrows raised high. "You've got another one."

"Another one?"

"That carving of a man carrying a boy on his shoulders."

Too late, Ethan remembered that he had left it standing in a corner beside his tool bench, half-hidden by bins of dried food. Unfinished, flawed, the faces all wrong.

"Um, yes. A failed experiment."

"Failed? Hoo boy, Ethan, it sure doesn't look like a failure. Sad, though. The father's face is really sad. The boy looks scared."

"Well, yes, that's why. I tried to make them smile. I'll get back to it someday."

No more was said for the time being, because the supper was now bubbling on the Primus, threatening to spill over. Ethan busied himself filling two large bowls with stew.

They ate more or less in silence.

"The dolphin," Ross said as they sipped at their cups of tea. "Are you going to paint it?"

"Eventually."

"Can I make a suggestion?" Without waiting for a reply he went on, "I think you should leave it unpainted. You could oil it with linseed oil, or olive oil, if you have it. That would bring up all the wood tones. Painted, it would be folk art. Unpainted, it would be pure art— actually, *fine* art."

"You may be exaggerating, Ross."

"No," he said with a somber look. "No, I'm not."

Changing the subject, Ethan asked him how long it would take to install the turbine. Ross thought it would probably take half a day, maybe a day at the most, if there were no unforeseen problems. Then he launched into a mind-boggling description of components that Ethan tried to follow without much success.

"A tower is usually best," the boy concluded. "That's what most people use. But you already have super wind access everywhere on the island. How about I put it on the roof of the work shed? That way, we'll use less wire. I can install the batteries in some spot below in the shed, rig up the inverter, the controller, the disconnect switch, what have you, and then wire the circuits for the shed and cottage—a few light fixtures and maybe one plug-in wall socket for each. I've brought you a box of low-energy LED bulbs, yellow end of the spectrum, like daylight. Hundred watt and sixty watt—translates into about eighteen and ten watts energy draw."

Uneasy again, Ethan wondered what the boy had paid for all of this.

"This is expensive," he said reprovingly.

"Hey, Ethan, you gotta stop worrying so much. Like I said, it's a gift."

"Ross, I hardly know you."

"You hardly *know* me?" said the boy, looking astonished, and perhaps a little hurt.

"Strangers don't do this kind of thing."

"Is there a law that says they can't? Anyway, I'm hardly a stranger."

Ethan dropped his eyes and frowned. It did not add up. It made no sense.

"*And*, Mr. McQuarry, if you're wondering if this comes with price tags of the social kind, just relax. I'm not going to use this as a bargaining chip so I can move in or make you my summer cottage every year." He laughed. "I promise I won't be invading your life."

Ethan kept shaking his head, captivated by the benefits the generator would bring but still concerned about hidden costs.

"But why?" he asked.

"You've heard about drive-by shootings? Random acts of violence? Well, this is a random act of kindness."

"Kindness."

"Yeah, and if that makes you uncomfortable, I assure you it's *your* kindness to *me*. The fact is, I always wanted to live in a lighthouse. I'll never get to do it, so please allow me a little vicarious pleasure."

"You should be a lawyer."

"Ha! I rest my case."

In the morning, Ethan got his wooden ladder out of the shed and leaned it against the roof. After that, he helped Ross carry the turbine's base frame, a stainless steel structure, up to the peak of the roof.

Once again, Ross had come prepared. He had brought a fully charged battery drill, and with this he drilled the bolt holes for securing the frame to the peak. When it was firmly installed, another hole was drilled for the wires that would connect to the batteries below. After that, they climbed back down to the boxes of material and sorted through them for the rotor, generator, and tail.

"Wide-sweep rotor," Ross said, in instruction mode, "which means a higher amount of energy produced. The tail keeps the turbine facing into the wind at all times."

Then came the three fiberglass blades, which they bolted onto the rotor after locking it in safety position. There was a fair breeze coming in from the east, and Ross warned that the blades could deliver a nasty clip.

Next, the wiring was fed through the hole and connected to the various apparatuses below.

Finally, Ross went topside again, carrying a tube of sealant in a caulking gun. He filled every crack and scrambled back to earth with a look of satisfaction.

"There," he said. "Neither rain nor snow nor sleet nor hail can deter us from our course. Should be good for years. I'll leave the gun with you, in case you ever need it."

After lunch, Ross went back down to his boat and returned with a spool of coated copper circuit wire. Comparing notes with Ethan, he installed the circuit from the batteries to the shed's rafters, wiring in three metal boxes for the ceiling fixtures, and a fourth at the base of an upright beam, for a plug box. The fixtures were added with little effort.

Then he drilled a hole through the shed wall into the cottage storage room. More wiring followed, which allowed for a single ceiling light in each of the three rooms, plus an additional plug box in the kitchen, and wall switches for each.

"Done," said Ross, screwing lightbulbs into sockets.

"You work very quickly," Ethan commented.

"Last year I helped my dad build our garage. I wired the whole thing myself."

The boy disappeared for a time. Ethan diced onions and threw them into a frying pan, along with crumbled hamburger. He set a pot of rice to boil. Peering out the window, he noted the sky turning deeper blue and whitecaps on the ocean.

Without warning the bulb in the ceiling went on, throwing artificial daylight into every corner. Light poured from the two side rooms.

Ross was soon back in the kitchen.

"Everything's going as planned," he said. "Propellers are spinning, lights are on in the shed."

"It's astonishing," said Ethan, walking from room to room, flicking switches off and on.

"Didn't I tell you?"

Ross went out again, returning within minutes, carrying a small portable electric heater, the size of a toaster.

"We'd better test the limits," he said, plugging it into the kitchen wall socket. The heater's elements began to glow a soft orange. Almost immediately the ceiling light dimmed.

"It's a huge drain," said the boy. "It's ceramic, energy efficient, but it takes five hundred watts. The batteries are probably low and need to be charged to maximum. If this wind keeps up, it may be possible to run lights and heater together." He flicked off the lights in the side rooms, and after doing the same in the shed, he crouched down by the heater and observed it.

"A little better but not by much," he muttered.

When he unplugged the heater, the kitchen light glowed to full luminosity.

"Let's let it charge overnight," he said. "Tomorrow we'll know for sure."

They exchanged technical talk as they ate supper, Ethan learning a few things about alternative energy sources and their maintenance. They lingered long over their cups of tea, Ross asking about the activities of seals and whales in the nearby waters, about fishery problems, the striped bass, and so forth. Before they knew it, night was looming. Ethan switched on the diesel generator for the beacon and went up to the watch room. Ross switched off the lights fed by the wind generator, allowing the batteries to charge fully. He chose to remain in the kitchen, reading a manual of some kind.

The wind had declined overnight, but clearly it had charged the batteries sufficiently to power the lights and the little heater, which ran well in tandem after everything was switched on. Even so, some loss was detectable within an hour, though things picked up again as the wind increased.

"Well, the heater's for winter," said Ross. "With enough wind and only a light or two on at a time, it could work. I mean, if your main source of heat fails, that is."

Together they went out to the shed to check on the apparatus.

"Everything looks good, Ethan. But we should have given more thought to organizing things. Dolt that I am, I placed these batteries plunk in the middle, and you could trip over them in the dark. Also, they're blocking space for some big project you might need to do in here."

"True," said Ethan. "But I have no big projects in mind."

"Why don't we move that cupboard over to the other wall, and shift the battery array to where the cupboard's standing now?"

Moving it would be no small challenge, Ethan knew. It was a formidable piece of furniture. Moreover, it was full of secrets.

"It's an old sea locker, not a cupboard," said Ethan. "I'm guessing it came from a schooner in the 1800s, floated up after the ship was wrecked. There are names scratched on the sides, sailors' names, I think. And just along the top panel you can still see a few words cut into the wood: *Good Ship Cutty Burhou*."

"Quite a history! An antique, really, so we'll have to move it carefully."

"No, it would be too heavy."

"Are you sure? I'll bet the two of us could do it."

Without waiting for an answer, Ross strode over to the locker and opened its doors.

"Whoa, whoa, whoa," he exclaimed, slapping a hand to his forehead. "What's this?"

And *this* led to the next project. Somehow Ethan got over his sensitivity regarding his self-created family, and somehow Ross convinced him that these "masterpieces" would steadily go downhill if they did not have a dry, warm residence of their own.

By now Ethan was used to Ross's wheedling ways. He saw it all coming, the eager enthusiasm, the flattery, and the ever-so-reasonable argumentation. Pausing for an intake of perspective, he drew back a little, wondering in the privacy of his thoughts who this boy was and how on earth, or on sea, he had moved into his life. He was prepared to resist; he would be firm; he would be unshakable. Nevertheless, in the end he capitulated, admitting to himself that the shed was largely unused and that the modification of part of it to make a clean and spacious workshop for his carving would be a boon. Moreover, it would free up space in the cottage.

So they spent the rest of the day at the kitchen table, discussing what would be needed.

"It looks to me like your diesel tank and the generator take a third of the space, on the left side, closest to the tower," said Ross. "That means you could build the shop on the right, in the space up against the cottage wall, leaving a twelve-foot-by-twelve-foot center section that can stay as it is, just a shed for some big project, like building another boat. Does this sound good?"

After some mental picturing of the proposal, Ethan said, "It sounds good."

"Now, to recap: The shed is roughly thirty-six feet wide and twelve feet deep—I paced it off. And if you build your new workshop sixteen feet wide and twelve feet deep, you'd have a pretty big room to work in."

"Yes, it will be excellent in summer."

"I mean all year round. You do your carving mostly in winter, am I right?"

"Yes, from fall to spring."

"So, I suggest we invest in insulation, add a few more wall plugs, a baseboard heater, et cetera—"

"*We*? Here I draw the line, Ross. You can be the architect, but *I* will do the investing. I will pay for all materials. Otherwise, we can forget the project now."

Ross sobered, examining Ethan's face. "All right," he said, and then with a smile, "You win."

"And something for your labor."

"Sorry. You lose on that one. Otherwise, we can forget the project now."

"Mmm."

"Yup, *mmm*. So, Ethan, should we, due to our intransigent difference of opinion, become double losers?"

"Put that way, Ross the Negotiator, I can accept a compromise."

"Then we'll both be winners."

"Still, I don't understand what's in it for you. You can get experience anywhere."

"I'm in it for the fabulous meals you serve."

The debate completed, they set their minds to writing down the materials they would need for the building project, from nails to wall panels to insulation, and a fair bit more.

The following day, they took both boats into Brendan's Harbour. The sky was lowering with a threat of rain, but there was little wind. At the building supply store, which, fortuitously, had been added to the hardware store a year ago, Ethan purchased everything they would need, while Ross checked items off the list one by one. For a nominal fee everything would be delivered to the wharf.

"Almost three thousand dollars in total, Ethan," said the boy as they waited on the dock for the delivery truck. "I hope you knew what you were getting into."

"I had a rough idea. Not to worry. Money is basically meaningless."

"Uh, well ..."

"The *Puffin* is broader of beam than your Lund. How about we load all the plywood panels into her, and the two-by-fours into yours. Each of us can take a few bales of insulation. Other odds and ends we can divide wherever they fit."

"Yeah, that'll work."

Ross went off for a while, explaining that he had a couple of chores to do in town. He was back soon enough, carrying plastic grocery bags.

The delivery truck arrived. So far, the rain clouds had kept themselves in check, and all the materials were loaded into the boats and covered with new plastic tarps. The whole was battened down with bungee cords.

An hour later, they tethered the boats to the island quay and began offloading. Then came the task of carting it all up the slope to the work shed. The dozens of four-by-eight sheets of plywood were the hardest going, as only a few could be carried at a time, considering their weight and cumbersome size. All of them were inside the shed just as a few drops fell out of the sky. By the time a light rain had begun, the insulation bales and the last of the lumber were safely under cover.

"Nice timing," said Ross.

"A job well done," Ethan replied.

"This'll take a week at least," said Ross with an apologetic look. "Can you put up with me for that long?"

"Slave labor is hard to come by these days."

"Uh, do you mind if the slave makes supper tonight?"

"I was planning sardines on toast, and a can of pork and beans."

"That sure sounds delectable, Ethan, but how about I take a turn?"

Ethan smiled ruefully. "Sure, why not?"

The banter continued off and on throughout the remainder of the afternoon.

Supper was fried steak and onions, steamed fresh vegetables with Indonesian seasoning, and a green salad with garlic dressing. The cottage had never smelled so good, Ethan decided. He also tried out a glass of red beer from a can provided by his guest, who drank a full one of his own. He had never liked drinking, due to its chronic associations with his childhood and youth. But in all truth, the mellow feeling the beer gave him was well worth the overcoming of prejudices or imprinting or whatever it was. Soon he was smiling and chuckling for no reason at all, the sweet temper appearing out of nowhere from the core of his stoic vigilance. When Ross told an amusing story, Ethan guffawed.

"Looks like you've had enough, buddy," said Ross with a mock censorious squint. "Whew, and only on one beer. Well, you get another one tomorrow, if you work hard."

Which made Ethan belly laugh. This was unprecedented, and embarrassing, though it felt good.

Ross asked if he could spend a couple of hours in the tower during Ethan's shift. Up in the watch room they chatted awhile over the shop they would build, and then scanned the night horizon for ships. After that, Ross browsed his way curiously through the books stacked in piles around the walls.

"Eclectic," he said.

Ethan looked up the word in his dictionary and could not help but agree: his reading material ranged from engineering to poetry; wood carving to small engine repair; mathematics to birds—and novels, chronicles, histories, tide books, and manuals for marine radio.

They tested the foghorn, which Ethan had rarely used in all these years. It was shockingly loud, vibrating every cell of their bodies, and doubtless scaring away whales. Both of them agreed that it should be used only if an oil tanker were about to crash into the island.

The next morning over breakfast, Ross said with a sheepish look, "I must've sounded kind of flip last night, about the beer and everything. I didn't mean to be disrespectful."

"I didn't think you were disrespectful," Ethan replied, surprised.

"Beer does that to me, you see, makes me say all sorts of ridiculous things. Like, I wanted to jump to my feet after supper and salute you, and deliver a solemn honorific. A *paean*, really."

"What is a paean?"

"A kind of praise. I was going to declare, 'O my noble captain, you are admirable and brave, a true man.' Something like that. Then you started belly laughing, which kind of ruined the mood."

"I appreciate your sense of humor, Ross."

"Most people don't. Mix a little alcohol into my kind of wit, and then they *really* don't get it. I'm amazed you do."

"Well, we don't get many wits landing here on the island."

"Wow, truly desolate. Witless on Castaway Island."

"Mmm," Ethan concluded. "I suppose we should get started, or you'll be stranded here forever."

"I'm your man Friday."

The Bell

For Ethan, the building of a home for his wooden family was an education. Though skilled in minor carpentry repairs, he had never before undertaken a construction project. He let Ross lead the way, following his directions. Much of the time they worked side by side without a great deal of discussion, instinctively taking up the pattern they had established the previous summer when launching the *Puffin*.

It took a day and a half to build the new floor, using Ethan's barely sharp handsaws, which was the time-tested method but slow going. Then they stuffed insulation between the joists and covered them with plywood sheets. In addition, after removing Ethan's wooden family from the sea locker, they maneuvered the giant piece of furniture up a temporary ramp and onto the floor.

The next two days were spent building wall frames and erecting them, using handsaws, hammers, and nails.

The day after that, Ross occupied himself drilling holes in wall studs for wiring, and connecting the circuits to the existing power source, the diesel generator. He also rewired the lines from the wind generator. A baseboard heater was added, along with plugs on three of the walls. Ethan focused on building a frame for the cottage wall, single-handedly, now that he had learned how it should be done. He had discussed with the boy whether this was needed, and they had surmised that the degree of insulation in the old cottage was probably minimal, maybe just sawdust that would have settled over time, or maybe nothing at all. They concluded that the new room should be completely padded for maximum retention of warmth.

"I don't want to run the diesel during the daytime," said Ethan. "For one thing, it's too noisy, and for another, it would raise the fuel consumption per year, and I couldn't justify it to my superiors."

"Understood, Ethan. That's why we should insulate as well as we can. Then, whenever you work here in daytime in chilly weather, you just switch to the wind generator; you use the plug-in heater instead of the baseboard and stay plenty warm to do your carving."

"Like a thermos bottle."

"Right, but better."

So up went the fourth wall, snug against the cottage.

"There really should be a door through to your pantry," Ross said. "Better to do it now than later. It'd cost a few hundred dollars more, but, what the heck, it's your money, and money is basically meaningless, right?"

"Right."

"Can we take the *Puffin* into town and pick it up?"

"Let's go."

At the building supply store, Ethan purchased a door and frame and the necessary hardware. Throwing all discretion to the wind, he also bought a high-quality, double-pane window. Nor did he neglect to buy gallons of white paint and rollers.

"Light," he said by way of explanation.

"Absolutely," Ross replied with a nod of approval. "There's no living without it."

While they were waiting for delivery at the wharf, Ethan said he would go see if there was any mail for him. He and Ross walked two blocks along the shoreside street and went into the post office.

There was not much in his lobby box other than advertisements and two paychecks. Also a note from the postmistress, letting him know he had a parcel to pick up at the counter.

She handed it across to him, and as he inspected the return address he was happy to see that it was a shipment of new artists' paints he had ordered weeks ago. In the meantime, the postmistress had spotted Ross standing a pace or two behind him.

"Is this your little brother?" she asked Ethan with a coy look, emanating guile ... rather guilelessly.

"Um, no," said Ethan.

"I'm his hired hand," said Ross with a grin—the kind of grin that must have melted a thousand hearts.

"Ooh, you two look like you were joined at the hip. Had to separate you at birth with a chainsaw."

She set herself off into a cackling of mirth.

"Whatever," said Ross, dropping the grin, examining her with suddenly neutral eyes.

"And you got identical voices," she added.

"Huh?" said Ross.

"I don't think so," said Ethan, for their voices were quite unalike. Just as their physical appearance was markedly different.

He and the boy looked at each other, shook their heads, and left.

Ethan figured they had time to walk the four blocks in the other direction, to make his bank deposit. When that was done, they returned to the dock. The delivery truck soon arrived, and they carefully loaded the door and window into the *Puffin*.

Back on the island, they grabbed a hasty lunch and prepared for cutting a hole through the cottage wall. Ross had purchased a few items at the hardware store that he had long been intending to buy for himself but had never gotten around to until now. These included a carpenter's level, a plumb bob, extension cords, and an electric circular saw. He asked Ethan if he would mind turning on the diesel generator for a few hours. The remainder of the day was spent using the new saw, which screamed maniacally, cutting through the clapboards at the back of the work shed, making a large opening for the window. The greater challenge was in cutting through the shingles and external planks of the cottage wall. As suspected, there was little insulation other than sawdust that had settled low between the heavy old wall studs. Layers of yellowed newspaper had been rolled and wadded down in places.

"Time capsule!" Ross cried, extracting them carefully. "The Halifax *Chronicle Herald*."

He set them aside, and the work continued until the pantry room was exposed. Ethan and Ross stepped through the gap, well pleased by the day's work.

Over an after-supper cup of tea, Ross perused one of the newspapers.

"Oh wow, things are looking bad in Europe, Ethan," he said. "There's a nasty politician in Germany rearming his country, breaking treaties. A British politician named Churchill is warning everyone about it, but editorial opinion is that he's an alarmist—'hysteria', they're calling it."

"That sounds like 1933 or '34," Ethan mused. "The cottage must have been built around that time. Before then, I'm not sure where the keepers lived. There may have been a poorer cottage that burned down or was torn down. Or it could be they lived in the tower itself."

"Maybe it was built for a keeper who found himself a wife?"

"Yes, that's possible."

By the end of the following day, both the window and door had been installed, smoothly opening and closing.

The next morning, Sunday, Ethan woke as usual, and went outside to call Ross in for a late breakfast. He found the tent empty and the Lund missing. Early in the afternoon, he heard the approach of a motor and went down to the quay.

"You went to town?" Ethan asked as he helped the boy moor the boat.

"Yup," he said, and volunteered no further information.

They spent a few quiet hours on their own, Ethan napping and reading, Ross fishing off the quay with rod and reel. He caught a small sea bass and a larger salmon, over three pounds, which they ate for supper.

On Monday morning the work resumed. The insulation batts were installed between every wall stud and ceiling joist, and plastic sheeting stapled over them as a vapor barrier—a few hours' work. After that, the plywood panels went up on the walls and ceiling. Their knotholes added a homey look, and the spruce veneer infused the space with a refreshing aroma.

On Tuesday, after Ross stapled plastic sheeting to cover the floor temporarily, they painted the room's interior. While the first coat dried, Ross took it upon himself to employ his circular saw out in the shrunken shed, ripping long narrow strips from leftover two-by-fours. With these, he would later trim the door and window. The paint was water-based latex and soon was ready for recoating. Both Ethan and Ross neglected supper in order to complete the project. When it was done, the room glowed with pristine beauty under the three ceiling lights. It looked like a *real* room, thought Ethan. Twelve feet by sixteen feet, which was more open space than he had ever lived in during his entire lifetime.

Looking at each other they began to laugh, for both were spattered head to toe with speckles from the paint rollers. Faces and hands were visibly the worst, but there was also the "atmosphere" of days of sweat.

"Time for a shower," said Ross.

"Sorry, no shower in this establishment," said Ethan.

The sun had just slipped below the horizon when they went down to the cove with towels and a bar of soap. It had been the first hot day of the year, and in the shallows the water was pleasantly warm. They bathed and scrubbed, swam out of the cove to rinse themselves, returned to shore, and scrubbed some more. Finally, dried off and refreshed, they dressed in clean clothes and walked up to the cottage in the dark. After a quick bite of food, Ross yawned and said he needed to catch up on his "sleep debt" and headed off to his tent. Ethan went up to the watch room and read for a time. In the middle of the night, he returned to the cottage to peer through the pantry door, and gazed at his new workshop with something like wonder.

"Ethan," said Ross, bleary-eyed over pancakes and maple syrup, "how about we let the paint cure for one more day? I can put up the trim tomorrow. Varnish the floor too."

"We *have* been going pretty steady. Yes, we could use another day of rest."

"I was thinking more along the lines of recreation. You mentioned a place called Wreck Isle. I might try diving there. It'd wake me up. Can you give me directions?"

"I can give you directions, if you want to go alone, but I'd be glad to take you there."

"Even better!"

The Lund was ideally suited to the sojourn, faster and lighter than the *Puffin,* her metal hull better able to take any unforeseen encounters with shoals or solid flotsam. Though Ethan knew the waters there fairly well, he kept a sharp lookout at the bow. The tide was low, and the danger greater. The island was a mile or so away, and soon they were circling it.

Wreck Isle was hardly an island. In fact, it was a projectile of black rock less than thirty feet wide at low tide. No living thing grew on it save mollusks. At high tide it was invisible, its guano deposits daily washed away. Between it and the mainland there was a narrow channel through which a fishing trawler would safely pass but no larger boat could survive. The water depth was only three to four fathoms over a cruel array of granite teeth. Embedded in these was the wreck of the old sailing ship that had foundered in a century long past. Whatever remained of it gave testimony to a severe impact, and a subsequent beating and shattering that had left little but the great keel beam and the remnant of ribs that had settled permanently between jaws in the undersea landscape.

Ross cut the motor, and Ethan let down the anchor chain.

"Three fathoms to the bottom, by the looks of it," Ethan said. "There's not much left of her."

"I'm going down there," Ross declared. "I've got to see."

He kicked off his shoes, peeled off his T-shirt, and, wearing only his khaki shorts as swimming trunks, slipped his feet into long blue fins and donned a black diving mask. Then on went the scuba tanks and mouthpiece.

"See ya later," he said, and flipped his body backward out of the boat.

Ethan quietly waited, unable to observe what was happening below. He watched the oxygen bubbles breaking the surface of the dark waves, worrying a little, impressed by the inexhaustible versatility of human courage. The bubbles appeared regularly, however, so he supposed that all was well.

Fifteen minutes later, according to Ethan's wristwatch, Ross's head appeared. He spit out his mouthpiece, flipped the mask up over his brow, and clung to the gunwales with both hands.

"Oh wow, Ethan," he gasped. "What a ship she must have been. Like you said, there's not much left, but you can see the incredible mastery that went into building her."

"How is the water?"

"Cold. Invigorating. Lots of fish and crabs down there. And I've found something very interesting. There are bits of metal here and there, iron spikes and strapping, all very rusted and covered with algae and barnacles. And something else. I'm going to try bringing it up. Can you hand me that cable?"

Coiled beneath the stern seat was a length of climber's rope, braided blue nylon, half an inch thick.

"There's forty feet of it," said Ross, "which should be plenty. Would you feed it to me as I go down, and make sure you don't let go of the end?"

Ethan nodded, wondering what undersea treasure was in the offing.

Ross wrapped one end of the rope around his forearm and dove again. As Ethan let the rope slide through his hands, he kept his eye on the coil as it steadily unlooped. When the rope slackened and grew still, he tied his end around a metal thwart and secured it with a sailor's hitch.

Not long after, Ross's head reappeared, and he heaved himself out of the water and rolled into the boat.

After shedding his diving gear, he knelt by the cable and began to haul it in.

"It's not all that heavy," he said.

"So, it's not a treasure chest."

"Nope, but a treasure nonetheless."

Finally the mysterious object tied to the end of the cable broke the surface, the size of a melon, green with slime.

When it had been pulled into the boat, dripping and smelling of fish and rank vegetation, Ross said:

"Covered with cyanobacteria, of course, but none the worse for wear."

"It's a bell," murmured Ethan with fascination, examining the object's shape. "The ship's bell."

"Uh-huh, not a big warning bell for fog, so it must have been the bell for changing shifts, night and day watches, or calling crew to the galley and things like that."

Ross wiped some of the slime away, revealing a patch of black metal.

"It looks like tarnish, not rust. This bell was cast from something that's resisted corrosion. Not brass, obviously, which corrodes badly in salt water. You can still see letters on it."

"Can you read them?"

"No, we'll have to give this a good cleaning, and then we'll find out more. I think it's silver."

Upending it, he noted, "The clapper's intact."

He shook the bell, resulting in a dull *thug-thug* sound.

After they beached in the cove, Ross carried the bell up to the cottage.

"It's substantial and was probably expensive to make, even in those years," he said. "Maybe it was the captain's bell. Maybe he built the ship or owned it ... By the way, do you have any aluminum foil and baking soda?"

"Both," said Ethan.

The process of cleaning the bell took a good while, but Ross seemed dedicated to doing it carefully. At the kitchen sink, he repeatedly bathed the bell with boiling water, and gently scrubbed away all organic growths with a soft cloth, explaining that hard scrubbing could scratch the surface.

"It's silver, all right," he said after the fourth bath, smiling at the black bell that had emerged from its encrustations.

He then lined the sink with aluminum foil and set the bell on top of it.

"We're going to make a nice little nuclear bomb," he said with a sly look at Ethan. "Actually, an electrochemical reaction."

He poured a gallon of boiling water over the bell, totally immersing it. To this he added a cup of baking soda and stirred it in with a wooden spoon. Immediately the mixture began frothing. He let it stand for a few minutes, saying, "The kind of silver polish you buy in stores often has an abrasive in it, which removes some of the silver and can leave scratches. By contrast, this method leaves the silver intact and just removes the tarnish. It's the slow method but the sure one."

"I'm not sure I understand," said Ethan, admiring the boy's knowledge but wanting no more than the basics.

"Believe it or not, Ethan, there's a small electrical reaction being produced here. The silver sulfide, or tarnish, releases sulfur atoms, transferring them to the aluminum."

"How do you know such things?" Ethan asked with a shake of the head.

"I learned it at my mother's knee—and other low joints."

After draining the sink and rinsing, Ross repeated the whole procedure. The bell was beginning to look somewhat less gloomy though still had a brownish tint.

"Can you read the words yet?"

"I could, Ethan, but I'm restraining myself. Let's wait till she's ready."

More bathings followed.

By the end of the afternoon, the bell was glowing brightly. A few dark pinholes were visible on its surface, but otherwise it looked astonishingly new.

Ross lifted it up by the silver loop on its peak, and shook it. It gave forth a sonorous *tang-tang-tang*, reverberating like rings of audible light.

After rinsing the bell with a final pot of boiling water, Ross let it cool, and then Ethan dried it with a towel, placing it in the center of the kitchen table.

Ethan and Ross stood still, hesitating.

"You read it," said Ross.

"No, you read it; it's your bell."

The boy bent over and read aloud the letters inscribed around the bell's waist.

"*Cutty Burhou*, it says."

Ethan peered closely.

"Yes, it's *Cutty Burhou*."

"And an angel," said Ross, pointing to a winged figure inscribed above the name.

"Now we know—the sea locker came from the wreck."

"Which means it's *your* bell, Ethan."

Before Ethan could voice a protest, Ross hastened out of the room, tossing over his shoulder a hasty "I'll be back in a flash."

A minute later, Ethan heard the Lund's outboard gunning off into the distance.

The flash lasted three hours or more. By the time Ross returned, night had fallen and the diesel generator was on, the beam arcing back and forth over the open sea. He had brought back a big box of pizza and a sack of canned beer.

As they ate their late supper and sipped beer, Ethan said, "That was a long way to go for a luxury meal."

"Pizza ain't luxury, Ethan; pizza's a staple of life. Besides, the bell's worth a celebration, don't you think? What's more, I popped into the library, and the lady in charge let me use the internet. You know what the internet is, don't you?"

"I think so. I've heard of it."

Ross laughed.

"Anyway, I did some research into online chronicles of nineteenth-century shipping, and I found out quite a bit about our wreck. It turns out she was a clipper ship, used for transporting tea in the 1800s before the advent of steamships. She was named for one of the Channel Islands, Burhou, which lies between England and France—just like the *Cutty Sark*, which was named after Sark, one of the other Channel Islands. The *Burhou* went down in 1869, with one survivor, a cabin boy named Fraser Chartrain. That's all the company's records showed—other than their obvious overfocus on the loss of a valuable shipment. There was an obituary for the crew but nothing about what happened to the boy afterward, or where exactly the ship had foundered."

"If they knew the boy was a survivor, surely they would know where the ship went down."

"The records said only, 'Off the coast of Nova Scotia.'"

"Even so, we've learned a lot."

"One more thing, Ethan," Ross added with an eager look. "I did some more surfing, looking for the island of Burhou, and what do you know! It's uninhabited, so the survivor couldn't have come from there. He was probably just a lad hired on in Guernsey or Jersey, since both of them have big towns. Anyway, Burhou is pronounced *ber-roo*, or *brew*, which is why I brought you some more of your favorite beverage. And another important detail: Burhou is only a bit bigger than your island, and it's the nesting ground for a colony of puffins."

"Well now!" exclaimed Ethan with a large smile.

The final stages of work resumed the next morning. Ross trimmed the door and window, giving the room a finished look. He then proposed cutting a few of the wide, thick pine boards, which from time out of memory had floored a part of the work shed attic, above the diesel generator.

"They look old, Ethan," he said. "They'd do nicely for shelves around your carving room. That way you can display your medium-size pieces. I can also make shelves that would fit inside the sea locker, so you can store the smaller ones. What do you say?"

"I'd appreciate it, Ross. Yes, it would complete everything, and be better protection for the carvings."

So Ross put his hand to bringing the old planks down to the room, and cutting lengths with his circular saw.

Around noon, they took a break for a bite to eat and a cup of strong tea.

"You've been here more than two weeks, nearly three, Ross," said Ethan. "I'm concerned about your research project."

"Oh, no worries there. My project should take no more than a month, maybe six weeks at the most, and the summer's just beginning."

"You've been giving a lot of your life for my sake."

"No way, this is fun."

"A random drive-by—"

"A random act."

When they had returned to work, Ethan said, "Your family must be wondering where you are."

"They know I'm okay. I dropped them a line last time I was in Brendan's Harbour for supplies."

"That's good."

"My mother's a terrible worrier, you see. If she didn't hear from me, she'd have the whole province turning over stones in search of my dead body."

"And your father?"

"My stepfather's a sensible guy. He's great, keeps Mum from going off the deep end."

"Stepfather?"

"Yeah, I never knew my real father. Single-parent situation, you know."

"Oh. I'm sorry."

And he *was* sorry, since his own circumstances were similar—minus the stepfather. He now thought of his mother and wondered, as he had countless times, where she was. Had she straightened out her life, gotten married, settled down, kicked the booze and other habits? Or died of them? Had she tried to find him, as he had tried to find her? In the end it came down to the truth that she had not been capable of bearing the weight of a child through life, of raising him. He was not wanted. Knew he was not wanted very early on. Though something in him understood that she had *wanted* to want him.

She gave me life. She did her best.

"No need to be sorry for me," Ross continued, after sawing another length of plank. "I've been privileged. A good stepdad from age three onward, uncles and a grandfather before that. A lot of people pulled together after my mother conceived me, gave her the help she needed." He grinned and threw his arms wide. "And here I am!"

Ethan smiled at the theatrical declaration, and then occupied himself with a search for a missing tool, since he wanted no probes for reciprocation. *And where are your parents?* the boy would ask next. He couldn't answer that, and he couldn't lie. He had avoided some truths in his life, but he was pretty sure he'd never told a lie. He wouldn't start now. But the pain was too much.

"Where did that crowbar get to?" he murmured as he left the shed for the tower, where he rummaged around for half an hour until memories had run their course. Remembering the fatherless feeling, the longing to be picked up and tossed into the air and caught with a laugh, and carried on a shoulder ride as his father-protector strode fearless through the world. Remembering also how easily he might have grown up lopsided, gone in bad directions, but didn't, because there had been a few good men scattered throughout his childhood. He thought of a social worker when he was four years old, who looked him straight in the eyes and said, "Ethan, things are hard for you at home right now. But I can see as plain as day that you're going to grow up solid and true." And meant it. And Ethan believed him.

Later, there was a teacher who had praised his little stories and poems. "You really look at things, don't you, Ethan. And you think about them too." Then there was the gym instructor who patiently taught him basketball skills after class, encouraging him with every inch of progress, treating his failures lightly. "Try again, Ethan. That's right, that's right, now you're getting it." And the manager of a supermarket where he worked as a pack boy, giving him a bonus because he was always on time and worked harder than anyone else. "You're dependable," he said. And the counselor at a boys' club run by a church, his parting words when Ethan's mother decided to move them to another part of the city, his hands firm on the boy's shoulders, eye to eye, saying, "Ethan, you'll be a good, strong man."

And he believed this too—feeding like a starving child on the definition of himself, the shapes that manhood might take. These men stole nothing from him and gave him everything, the affirmation he hungered for. The quantity of such encounters had not amounted to much, but their quality was of immeasurable value.

Ethan returned to the new room.

"Did you find the crowbar?" asked Ross.

"No."

"Don't worry," he said with a smile. "I got it for you—sitting on that pile of boards."

"You really look at things, don't you," Ethan said. "And you think about them too."

"Oh, I don't know ...," the boy demurred.

"You're dependable."

To which Ross did not reply, though a flush of pleasure lit up his face.

"What about a workbench?" Ross said. "We've got some two-by-fours and plywood left over, enough for a countertop and tool rack."

"It's a good idea," said Ethan, hesitantly, after some thought. Yes, he could move his tools out here, freeing up space in the cottage.

"Would you like me to make you one?" asked Ross.

"It's more work. You've already done so much. And shouldn't you be getting on with your research project?"

"I've already answered that argument. Plenty of time left."

Running out of objections, Ethan tried one more time: "I could pay you for it."

"No need to pay me. I'd like to."

"All right," Ethan murmured with a sober nod. Wondering too late if it sounded cold and ungrateful.

Later, as Ross cut plywood pieces for the workbench, Ethan used his handsaw to cut two-by-fours to proper lengths. When the saws fell silent during a break, the boy said quietly, as if to himself:

"You don't like people, do you."

Ethan looked up, a little startled.

"I like people," he said.

"I mean, you don't *love* people. Not really. You don't want them around."

He had no reply for this, and he mused silently on the question. He could see that the boy had meant no offense, since his tone implied an observation, not a criticism.

"It's a solitary life here," he said in self-defense. "It's my work. It's my home. I have no other."

"I know. But ..."

They resumed their sawing.

"I can understand," said Ross after a while. "I can understand if you'd like me to go away."

This brought Ethan to an abrupt halt. He laid down his saw, furrowed his brow, looked at his boots, and considered.

"I don't want you to go away," he said at last.

"The workshop's almost ready," said the boy. "You won't need me anymore."

"I won't need your help anymore, after it's finished. Yes, that's true. But I don't want you to go away."

Ross absorbed it silently. Ethan could see that he was thinking about it, deeply and at length. He said nothing in reply, and they turned away to the tasks at hand.

Later, sleepless and restless, Ethan realized that it was the most unguarded thing he had said in his life. Why hadn't he said, offhand, "Oh well, you can stay. There are other jobs I could use your help with"? Why the simple declaration: "I don't want you to go"? Why had he frozen up after that, his thoughts and words stalled at some kind of barrier, a breakwater maybe?

He liked the boy. He was congenial and, if the truth be told, a great help. It was more a case of not knowing how to deal with him: the habit of frequent verbal communication, the wit that invited counterwit, the starkness of his observations, those probing questions. In other circumstances and with other people, these qualities would be acceptable or admirable, or at least not invasive. But they had amassed into something that was confounding the order of Ethan's world, giving him the sense that one whole wall of his life had tumbled down and left him exposed.

Exposed to what? To a need for other people that he had never seen in himself before? A need for relief from loneliness? A need to unfold his own personality by reflection, by dialogue with a living human being not made of wood, and in this way come to new dimensions of his humanity? He did not know. He was not sure he cared to know. It would be easier if the boy went away and never came again.

Yes, easier. But would it be better?

A Place Where We All Can Live

The shelves were up, the workbench completed.

Ethan did a final sweeping of the new room, gathering sawdust and wood chips, splinters and errant nails. When the floor was thoroughly clean, Ross came in, knelt down, and began stirring a can of varnish. Ethan stood by the pantry door, watching him. He was still perplexed by the boy's presence, his inexplicable generosity—indeed, his goodness. Throughout his life, Ethan had experienced much betrayal, a frequent exposure to the unreliability of human nature. For this reason, he had resolved to be true to his word, to resist at all costs any failing in integrity. He understood that it was partly reactionary, partly a means of avoiding the mistakes of the past and the chaos of the world. But was his nature or character, or whatever it was, a solid thing? Was it his real self? He believed it was—or hoped it was—and yet at the same time he wondered what it was all for.

While Ross varnished the floor, Ethan went out to the tower. Upstairs in the watch room he went through his private notebooks. In one of them he found what he had been looking for, a quotation about tides and floods.

On the back of an old chart, he penned:

Ross:

On the full sea of life you are now afloat. May you always avoid the shallows and miseries, and with ever open heart take the flood that leads on to fortune.

With thankfulness beyond words,

Ethan McQuarry

He folded the chart and brought it down to the ground floor, where he stuffed it into a burlap sack.

The varnish was dry to the touch by late afternoon. After a supper of steaming hugger-in-buff, and a slow musing over the final beers, the evening was a subdued one. Ross seemed far away in his thoughts. No words were initiated by either of the two as they puttered about, the man carrying his carvings out to the shelves in the new room, the boy helping him with the heavier pieces. The silver bell was installed on the top shelf in the sea locker, its doors wide open for display.

"There, it's done," declared Ross as they stood side by side, admiring what they had made together.

Then followed a smile from the boy and an amiable whack on the back.

"Who could have foreseen it?" said Ethan.

A place for my wooden family, he thought. *A place where we all can live.*

"I hope you'll be happy here, Ethan. When I'm back in Halifax I'll be imagining you churning out masterpieces."

"Well, we'll see. In any event, you're taking the bell with you."

"Nope. It stays here. It belongs here."

"It belongs to you, since you found it and discovered its past."

"Sorry, Ethan. You can keep it or give it away, but I'm not taking it. It's part of your life."

Ethan shook his head, wondering how he could possibly win an argument with a person as stubborn as this.

There was an aimlessness to the next day. It was the usual routine, but there were no significant tasks to engage them. Ross went swimming in the cove, and afterward he used rod and reel to fish off the quay, but caught nothing. He tinkered with the electrical components he had installed. He climbed to the shed roof and carefully rechecked everything on the wind generator and probed for cracks in the drill holes. He resealed them with the caulking gun. In the afternoon, he lay on the grass near the puffin nests, an arm over his eyes, soaking up the sun.

Ethan brought his tools from the pantry and installed them on his new workbench. Later, he took a nap in his bedroom, and woke to the smell of cooking stew.

Ross had prepared a rather mundane supper, island style, out of cans. They ate in companionable silence.

"Can I tell you a story, Ethan?" the boy said as they drank their after-dinner tea.

"Of course."

Ross paused for a moment of reflection, then continued in a quiet voice:

"It happened last year when I was scuba diving off the coast of Gaspé, a couple of weeks before I stumbled onto your island the first time. You remember when we launched the *Puffin*?"

"I remember."

"Right. That was early summer, so the water was warm enough. I was exploring this undersea cliff face, maybe about forty feet down, taking samples of saltwater flora clinging to the rock. It was a beautiful day, sun shining, the water as clear as you can get at that depth." Again he paused. "You might not believe what I'm going to tell you."

"I will believe you."

"Anyway, there I was, happily scraping away at the cliff, when all of a sudden I got this powerful feeling that someone was watching me."

"Watching you?"

"Like an intelligent being was *looking* at me, not from above but from behind my back. I shook it off, told myself it was imagination, refused to turn around to check it out. I went on with what I was doing, but the feeling wouldn't go away."

"Were you frightened?"

"No, that's the strange part. It wasn't a scary feeling at all. More like that odd certainty you sometimes get when someone's looking closely at you—when you know you're being observed, even though you can't see him with your eyes. Do you know what I mean?"

"I do," said Ethan with a nod.

"Maybe we have faculties that aren't entirely conscious or physical, like an inner radar or sonar. Or maybe it's a faculty of the soul. Anyway, when I was finished collecting specimens, I stowed the sample tubes in my kit and turned around. And there, not twenty feet away, was a huge eye looking at me."

"Really, an eye?"

"As you can guess, I was pretty startled. I just froze, and then I saw that the eye was embedded in a mountain of flesh. It was a blue whale, hovering there, not swimming. I didn't move. I just kept looking and looking, kind of in awe. And he kept looking back, as if he were thinking about me. A few seconds later, he did a slow roll and slid away. It seemed like forever for that enormous body to pass me by, and then with a gentle sweep of his tail flukes he disappeared into the deep."

Ethan said nothing, absorbing it.

"I'm going tomorrow," said Ross.

Ethan groped in his mind for an adequate reply.

"I guess it's time," he said at last.

"I guess it's time," said Ross, and went off to his tent for an early sleep.

After breakfast, they carried tools and scientific equipment down to the Lund. The tent and other gear came next, carefully stowed by Ross. The boat looked considerably emptier than when she had first arrived.

"Well," said Ethan.

"Yup, well."

They shook hands.

But neither of the two seemed to know how to bring the departure to a tidy conclusion.

"You never told me much about your life," said Ross.

"You haven't asked me."

"Okay, I'm asking."

"What do you want to know?"

"Where's your family? Parents, siblings?"

"I'm like you were," said Ethan hesitantly. "I had a single mother."

Ross straightened and inspected Ethan's face.

"Well, it happens," Ross said. "There are a lot of people like us now."

"Yes, a lot."

"How's your mother doing?"

"I haven't seen her in many years. I've tried to find her, but ..."

"Oh. I'm sorry. And your birth father?"

"He went away when I was in the womb. I don't know who he was."

Ross looked genuinely grieved by this.

"That's pretty brutal," he said. "I know how it feels. My own birth father just disappeared into thin air—like he never existed."

"But your mother kept you, loved you."

"Yes, she did. I love her too. And as I told you before, my stepdad's a great guy. Couldn't have asked for a better father. Still, I wonder about the guy who's my biological father—whatever happened to him, is he still around somewhere, that kind of thing."

"Is it painful for you to think about?"

"No, not anymore. Now I just wonder who he was. I was angry at him when I was a teenager—you know, the Invisible Man—but that passed. I feel sorry for him more than anything. Maybe pity's a better word. And you?"

"I've felt angry in the past. Now it's only sadness."

"Yeah, Ethan, I can see you're sad. You look sad just about all the time."

Ethan struggled to find words to deflect the probe. He had opened up far too much, and now it was time to shut down.

"You know how I got over my teenage gloom?" Ross said. "Whenever I drifted into thinking about my origins, the old feelings rising up, analyzing myself to death, feeling abandoned, I just started praying for that guy. When I prayed for him, the mood went away, the sun started shining again. Of course, it takes practice. My dad taught me this."

"Your adoptive father?"

"That's right. And my mum still prays for my biological father all the time, whoever he was; she can't even remember his name after all these years."

Ethan averted his eyes and started looking around the beach for anything the boy might have neglected to pack.

They stood on the quay and shook hands a second time.

"Well, it's time t' sail beyond the sunset and the baths," said the boy with his wry grin.

"Thank you for your help, Ross. I couldn't have done it on my own."

"I'd really like to come back someday, if that's okay."

"That would be fine."

"Thanks for all the great experiences."

Ethan dipped his head in acknowledgment.

"Right," said Ross, suddenly all business. "Time to go."

"Wait," said Ethan. He knelt and opened a gunny sack he had ported down to the shore. "This is for you."

It was the dolphin carving. Unpainted. Oiled, glowing with natural tones. The boy received it into his hands, and cradled it, pondering its every detail.

"A gift," said Ethan.

Ross looked up, unable to speak. His mouth tried to form words of thanks, but failed. Somber of face, blinking rapidly, he stepped into the boat and carefully laid the carving in the folds of his sleeping bag, snugged against a thwart.

"And this," said Ethan, handing over the nautical chart on which he had penned his parting message. Ross slipped it under the carving, unread.

As Ethan untied the bowline and pushed him off, Ross fired the motor. He wheeled his boat on the water, leaving an arc of spume on the deep beyond the cove. Then he straightened out and headed directly south to the headland and Brendan's Harbour, to his future, to other people and other tasks.

Then came a final wave of his hand, his red windbreaker like a splash of paint on the kingfisher blue and the dome of cerulean above it, almost a quaint folk painting, the forms containing all that was essential, man suspended above the abyss, the water and sky elegant, the points of color making the whole greater than the sum of its parts, as a work of art should do.

As he watched the little boat diminish, Ethan felt anew all the losses he had known in his life. Yet he also pondered the truth that this boy, this stranger, had also suffered loss and had risen above it, like a dolphin leaping, a soul riding the waves.

Out of the fog of his past he remembered that the girl he had loved when he was sixteen had borne the same surname as this boy. And then, without knowing why, he felt the world turning, the universe revolving around the polestar, the stars leaving a thousand wakes of light. And when it had completed its round, when his heart ceased hammering and his thoughts steadied, he knew. He knew who this Ross was.

That autumn, Ethan received a brief letter from Ross, in which the boy thanked him again for the interesting experiences and good conversations. And, above all, for the gift of the dolphin and its rider. He described his graduate studies, his plans, his regrets that he would not be able to visit next summer. He had been accepted by an oceanography institute for a research expedition. His schedule was jam-packed, but he would try to get up to Cape Breton before too much more time passed. Maybe next year, maybe the year after.

"Keep the light burning," he signed off.

"Keep safe, out there on the deep," Ethan whispered, or thought, as he carefully folded the letter and saved it.

But a piece of paper seemed too frail a thing to moor their lives together, though he read it again and again.

Should he write to the boy? Should he spell it all out, present his case, itemize the evidence—when there was, in fact, no real evidence? Even so, it was something stronger than an intuition, more like a certainty. And if the hunch did prove to be true, what good would it do? Undecided, Ethan composed letters in his mind, the disconnected phrases appearing out of nowhere, emotions materializing into thoughts that failed to add up to a coherent whole:

How shall we reinvent the world?
How shall we learn to live, when there is no one there to teach
  us?
I was robbed as you were robbed.
There was no weather gauge within me.
There was then no tower set upon rock to guide me through
  night and storm.

Back and forth he argued with himself. Of course, it
might be no more than coincidence, the name Campbell,
which was one shared by thousands in the Maritimes. Or
it might be self-delusion, a yearning for a family of flesh,
not made of wood. Or was it his strange mind extending
his habit of conversing with imaginary beings?

Then, moving beyond pure feeling, he examined the
question more closely. He remembered the day when he
and the girl had fallen into their unplanned moment of
passion. He was sixteen years old at the time. It was after a
dance at the end of the school year, which placed the exact
week for him—the last week in June. And Ross had told
him his age and the month of his birth—the end of March.
Nine months between the two dates, the child of a single
parent, father unknown.

But if she was the same girl, why had she not told him
about her pregnancy? Now he recalled that shortly after
the moment of passion, his own mother had abruptly
departed, forcing him to leave Halifax for work in logging
camps, leaving no trail behind him.

Was there any coded evidence in Ross himself, were
there similarities in their appearance? They were not the
same height; the boy was at least a head taller. Then again,
their body frames were balanced in the same way, wide at
the shoulders and narrow hipped, though this was in no

way conclusive. Their faces were different, and yet the high cheekbones, and the blue eyes in which the whole iris showed, were like those of the girl he remembered. And he shared Ross's coloring, the thick sandy hair that stood straight up from the dome of his forehead like dry grass in an offshore breeze, though this characteristic was common among many young men. There was, too, the unruly swirl of hair at the nape of the neck, a little whirlpool on the left side, the same as his own. And there was their voices—the postmistress had said Ethan and Ross sounded like twins, though neither of them had believed her at the time. Now it struck him that a man cannot hear his own voice as it is heard by another's ear.

Ethan delayed and delayed, though he often murmured to himself variations of the wording he might use, and went so far as to make fitful starts with pen and paper. But he scrapped all the drafts, burned them on the beach with his wood shavings, watching the sparks rise into the heavens and disappear, for words could never explain the unexplainable, the depths of human hearts, the mystery of choices. No less than before, he wanted to beg forgiveness for the sequence of events that had given the boy three years of abandonment before another man came along and became for him what Ethan should have been. In the end, he dropped the idea altogether. He saw that Ross was happy and strong and intelligent, and he would do well in the world. Ross needed no sea anchor dragging at his stern.

After picking up his mail one day in October, Ethan dropped by the chandlery to pose a few questions, to do a little research of his own. Biggs was a repository of a vast amount of town gossip and history and thus the most likely source of lore.

"Did you ever hear of a ship that sank just north of here, named *Cutty Burhou*?" Ethan asked him.

Biggs stuck a pencil behind an ear and leaned on the counter.

"*Cutty Burhou*?" he said, frowning, shaking his head. "Not that I heard of, and I've lived here all my life. When did she go down?"

"In 1869."

"Funny name."

"Yes, like *Cutty Sark*."

"You mean the whisky? Now that *Cutty Sark* I know," he chuckled.

"So you never heard the name before?"

"Nah," Biggs said with a dismissive wave of the hand. "There's been wrecks all along this coast since Columbus and Cabot."

"Have you ever heard the name Chartrain?"

"Chartrain? There's no Chartrains living round here now, but one of my great-grandfathers was a Chartrain, and he was the only one. Married a Biggs. They had one child, my grandmother she was, and she married into the Rileys, and one of their girls, my mother, married back into the Biggses. My family's mainly Biggs, Moloney, and Riley. That old lady at the library's my cousin."

"I see. Do you remember your great-grandfather's first name?"

"Oh, that's easy enough. His name was Fraser. Fraser Chartrain. The name Fraser got passed down to a boy each generation after him. That's why I'm Fraser Biggs. Why are you asking?"

Before Ethan could answer, a customer broke into the conversation, needing help with selection of merchandise. Biggs, ever expansive, talked overlong with the man, and Ethan left the shop.

He returned the next day, carrying a bundle in his arms.

Biggs was standing behind his counter, in an irritable mood by the looks of him.

"Yer back. So what was that all about yesterday?"

"A piece of history, Mr. Biggs—in fact, your own personal history."

Ethan opened the sack and removed the silver bell from it. He placed the bell on the countertop.

"What's this?" said the chandler, peering curiously at the bell, with an undercurrent of suspicion.

So Ethan told him the story of the *Cutty Burhou* and how she sank. There was a little guesswork involved about the aftermath, but he thought it happened like this: A cabin boy had survived by clinging to wreckage until he was washed ashore on the lighthouse island. The lighthouse keeper had brought him to Brendan's Harbour, where people took him in and nursed him back to health. Then this boy from a distant land, half-French, half-English, with no home and kin, had been taken into someone's care and raised to manhood. He had chosen to stay, and in all likelihood he had become a fisherman.

Biggs gave this some thought, his brow furrowed, eyes looking back across time.

"Aye, my great-grandfather was a fisherman, like all of them back then."

"This bell came from his ship," said Ethan.

"Nah, it can't be. It looks new."

"You remember the lad who worked for me last summer?"

"The loudmouth? Sure."

"He dove to the bottom and found the bell, brought it back up, and worked hard to clean it. It's a gift for you. For you to remember your past."

Openmouthed, Biggs stared at Ethan, then lowered his head, unable to raise his eyes.

Quietly, Ethan stepped out of the chandlery, went down to the wharf, and took the *Puffin* home.

The Storm

A catastrophic piece of news reached Ethan by mail a week after his meeting with Fraser Biggs. In a letter from the maritime authorities he was informed that the lighthouse would be closed down as soon as an automated beacon could be built on the headland above Brendan's Harbour. It might be as early as next year, the year after at the latest.

In the same letter, Ethan was offered a position at another lighthouse farther up the coast on the west side of Cape Breton, far from the open Atlantic. If he accepted the offer, he would transfer there as soon as the new beacon became operational.

The unexpected disruption of his world hit like a storm in his soul. Unbelieving at first, then angry, and then mourning, his turmoil found no relief.

He disagreed on principle with the policy of closing lighthouses one after another. He believed that the human factor was crucial, and that while automated beacons were more efficient, they had their own shortcomings, with consequent dangers to seafarers. Oh, he understood the reasons for the change well enough. Though his lighthouse had been built in the 1800s, it had little historical significance. It had been situated where it was only because the island was the easternmost extension of Cape Breton into the Atlantic—a location more symbolic than practical. Even a century and a half ago, the headland would have been a better site. Moreover, the tower was a burden on the authorities—it was difficult to maintain and costlier than others.

Feeling that he had no alternative, Ethan wrote a reply, accepting the offer.

On one of his trips to the harbor that month, he noted that a cement foundation had been poured on the rocky heights above the town, and the framework for a metal building was under construction, though far from finished. It was ugly, and Ethan instinctively disliked it. From his tower watch room he often looked through his telescope at its tiny shape rising, shaking his head, remembering ice storms and record snowfalls that had knocked out all electric power on the coast, sometimes for weeks. And what if there was only a power cord connecting the new beacon to the province's electric grid? Would they be foolish enough to neglect installing a backup generator and batteries? And even with backup, how long would these last if Cape Breton were hit by a major storm? Perhaps a huge tank would be installed, holding enough fuel to power a generator for a month. Maybe someone had been hired in Brendan's Harbour to come to the rescue in the event the worst happened, a maintenance man, not a vigilant.

As time passed, no longer measureless, no longer eternal, Ethan felt a yawning chasm opening within him, the kind of fear that he thought he had left behind forever—an undertow of dread—the certainty that leaving this island would be a return to namelessness, and homelessness. He knew that he would survive in the new place, could do the job well enough, would work there for as many years as he could bear it. He tried to reassure himself that he could take his annual vacations on his own island, though his heart sank when he saw the futility of this, for two weeks a year was very little.

I could quit now.

The thought came without warning, with no pre-meditation. For a moment he was a man standing on a bridge over an abyss, impelled to leap for no apparent reason. Then common sense kicked in, and he weighed the factors involved—the factors necessary for his survival: He was too young for the old-age pension, which would guarantee him enough to eat, though not much else. If he clung to the job until retirement, he would receive a larger employment pension, and then he could make a permanent return to his island. But both pensions were more than twenty years away. And would he be allowed to return? Who would own the island? The Coast Guard? Or would it revert to Crown land? No trespassing?

It would be a long exile, and it seemed from this vantage point to be nearly unbearable.

But is my life my environment? he argued.

He knew that it was not so, or only partly so. His life was within him, regardless of his surroundings. He would survive, over there in that new place. But it would be a survival of endurance.

Throughout the remainder of autumn and the onset of winter, Ethan made a number of things in his workshop. It was spacious, warm, and well lighted, and the shelves gradually filled with little wooden marvels: A three-foot-long replica of the *Puffin*. Two or three smaller boats, toys really, brightly colored. They gave him respites of joy, though the joy was haunted by the knowledge that time was running out.

As he whittled and carved, dialogues with his lost son spontaneously arose in his mind, through which they wove together their severed lives.

Dad, let's build a boat together. And sail her together.
Yes, Ross, let's do it. But what about your education?
This is my education. You can teach me.

Dialogues with Catherine were of a different order, consoling in a way, but leaving him lonelier than ever, wondering why she had not returned.

There is not much within me, Catherine, that a woman would want to spend a lifetime with. I am a boring person.

Two souls become as one, Ethan, she replied. How could that ever be boring?

Do you make music now, out there in the world? he asked.

Yes, I'm making music now. But we two could make music here, playing it for the puffins and for the listeningness, the awakeness in existence.

Would it be enough for you?

Yes, it would be enough for me, she said, taking his hand, looking him in the eyes. Don't be afraid, Ethan.

I've been afraid all my life, Catherine.

And you've overcome fear all your life. I see you protecting children from the violence of the blind and cruel. I see you as a boy in a forest, felling trees. I see you pulling people from the sea when it is angry.

You are the first to look inside me, and you still wish to know me.

Yes, I still wish to know you. It is called love, Ethan.

Glancing across the room at his artificial wife, he felt a momentary guilt of infidelity, but she gazed at him as fondly as ever. He shook himself, forced a laugh, and turned his thoughts back to real work.

In mid-December, he collected his mail before Christmas, and thus he was able to read it before the actual season. For the first time in his life there were personal messages. There was one from the family he had met over on the other side of Cape Breton, the people with so many children. Addressed to *The Lighthouse Keeper, Brendan's*

Harbour, N.S., the envelope was large, packed with crayon and pencil drawings of sheep, goats, chickens, horses, dogs, and five little people waving at him—the cavalcade. The picture on the card was puzzling: a donkey crossing a barren desert with a golden box on its back, light shining from it, like a beacon.

There was a card from Ross too, a painting of a Christmas tree with multicolored lights atop a lighthouse tower. The note contained some news: he was engaged to be married. Included in the envelope were photos: Ross and a young woman cheek to cheek, beaming. Ross triumphantly holding up a giant lobster. The dolphin carving sitting on a mantelshelf above a fireplace. A family group, mother, father, six children of various ages, Ross among them, clearly the eldest. The mother's face was unmistakable. Though aged by the passage of more than twenty years, it was the girl he had loved.

Elsie sent him a jolly card, a Santa Claus at the wheel of a schooner. If the weather was good, she wrote, would he come for Christmas dinner at her place? Many of the family were coming home for it, and she would be so happy if he could join them. Ethan did some swift computation of tides and long-range weather forecasts and decided it would be impractical to accept the invitation. These were flimsy excuses, he knew, and beneath them was the real reason—his aversion to crowds. But he would drop by her place soon, to thank her and to explain.

Early in the morning of the next good day, he took the boat into the harbor. As always, Elsie was glad to see him, and immediately offered their ritual tea.

They commiserated over the looming closure of his lighthouse, Elsie lamenting the way the world was becoming so automated—*robotty*, she called it, *inhooman*.

With a wily look she changed the subject, saying that if he could be trapped long enough, she would give him a breakfast on the house, right now, no strings attached, no fee. He told her he would be grateful to fall into her trap. So he took the tea and the meal and her gentle observations of harbor activities, and her questions that never probed too deeply but showed that she cared about him. It was her way. She was like this with everyone. Not a policy, and certainly not a front—more a radiance from her heart.

He glanced up at the shelf where the little boat he had made as a memorial for her husband still held the most prominent position, side by side with fancy dishware and the purple starfish.

"Well, to be honest, now, Ethan," Elsie said while he was wiping his lips with a paper towel, "it *is* a bit of a trap. I've knit a ton of stuff for the church bazaar. It begins tomorrow, and would you kindly be willing to carry that box down to Saint Brendan's? This lot is too bulky for my old arms, not to mention the icy streets and my brittle bones."

So he did as she asked, depositing the box in the parish hall. There one of the ladies fussing over decorations got him setting up the folding tables. And after that, he was pressed into carrying a balsam Christmas tree over into the church proper. Going up the front steps, he noted that the new church looked very much like the old one, at least on the outside. The roof, the spire, and its cross were shining metal, no longer the rusty carapace that had once capped the structure. The wooden clapboards were painted white, the eaves and window trim bright red, the same as his lighthouse. The double doors were oak, shining with recent varnishing, not yet weathered.

Inside, Ethan deposited the tree near the entrance, leaning it against the back wall. After thrusting his nose into the thick branches to inhale their fragrance, he sat down

173

on the rearmost bench and took another deep breath. He had more business to do in town, but it wouldn't hurt to rest a moment before he went on his way. He had never been inside a church before. It had its own smell, like beeswax combined with pine pitch or crumbled bay leaves, a kind of perfume unlike anything he had ever come across before.

He looked upward to the great wooden roof beams and was pleased to see the new *Star of the Sea* hanging on a golden chain above the central aisle. *Peter's Bark* or *Norbert's Boat*. She was beautiful, he now realized. And perhaps she consoled some broken hearts. He felt very good about that, and was thankful that no one would ever know who had made it. It was enough to have done a thing that shifted the imbalance in the world. Some people stole, but others gave. Too many takers, and the boat capsizes; enough givers, and she rights herself. It was a matter of choice what kind of person you would be.

It was a curious-looking place. The hardwood floors and the freshly painted walls looked flawless. The pews seemed antiquated in design, but he knew they couldn't have come from the original church—replicas, he thought. The big table in front, raised on a platform, made the room like a town hall, though more serious in nature or purpose. From his years of reading he recognized the crucifix hanging on the wall above the table, though not the gold box beneath it. Nor the meaning of the flickering red candle beside it.

There was a *listeningness* here, not unlike that of the sea and sky, or perhaps the *awakeness* of the universe, the bigger ocean. Timelessness too. At one point he sensed the presence of someone with him in the church, and so strong was the feeling that he quickly looked all around him, thinking that Elsie had come to find him. But there was no one there. Strangely, he continued to feel that he was not alone.

Simultaneously, without reason, he wanted to let tears flow, but couldn't at first. When they came, they were silent. It had been so long since this kind of thing had happened, maybe twenty years or more. Were these the overflow of solace or the release of sorrow? He didn't know.

I will come here again. I will rest here from time to time. I will listen to the listening.

But he would do it when no one else was around. Churches, he knew, were for good people, normal people. Of course, the magazines these days were trying to make out that churches were full of the deluded, the repressed, the dangerous. There were more and more people like Esau Hurley, who had condemned the churches as nets full of rotten fish. Instinctively, Ethan knew that places like this were full of good people, maybe a few rotten fish among them, but not all, not even many. This was the home of people like Elsie.

At the same time, he felt that he had no place among them. He belonged neither to the haters nor to the good.

I am a mistake. I was not wanted when I came into this world. And still I belong to no one.

Yet he listened a while longer, and waited, and the sense of timelessness continued, as if he were afloat in a new dimension, along with inner stillness and the cessation of his painful thoughts. He knew that he would return.

He was not sure how he arrived at another decision, but decision it was, made without proper deliberation, but with certainty and peace. He closed the church door carefully against the weather and walked down to the harbor to check on the *Puffin*, which was rising and falling beside the dock, casting up slurs of freezing froth, though she was otherwise stable. He talked a little with the boatmen hanging about, declined their sips from flasks, inquired about their catches, and listened to their stories.

Next, he went to the bank. He had long ago ceased paying attention to what was in his account. His expenses had been few over the years, his salary steadily accumulating. Now he learned that more than $200,000 was sitting there, unused.

After that, he searched out a law office—the town now had three of them—and discussed with one of the lawyers the island and its future. He hired the man to initiate a legal approach to the maritime authority that ruled the lighthouses and perhaps owned the island itself. He also made a will.

By nightfall he was home, resolved and well content.

As the winter progressed, Ethan maintained the beacon and waited for a response to his proposal. In time, papers arrived in the mail, and there were documents to sign. The authorities had agreed to sell. The tower would soon have no real purpose for them, and the cottage was practically worthless. The island, too, had no commercial or scientific value. It was a bit of grass and rocks, undistinguished by flora and fauna that could not be found in greater abundance elsewhere. And thus Ethan wrote a shockingly large check for his lawyer to handle, and it was done.

He now charted plans for his future. Next autumn, when the automated beacon switched on its light, he would resign. There was still $80,000 left in his bank account, and this, along with the diminished keeper's pension, would enable him to survive the long years ahead. He intended to eke out his savings carefully, a little for the *Puffin*'s fuel, a little for artists' paints, a little for basic food, no luxuries. From now on, there would be books and magazines from the library only, no more paid subscriptions. And no more B and B, though a cup of tea with Elsie would be fine from time to time. He would try his hand at fishing again, rod and reel. Make a lobster pot or cast a net off the bluff. He would eat bird eggs in the spring, though not from his own beloveds. He would explore up the coast and gather eggs from the breeding colonies of seabirds along the shore.

He would collect driftwood for the woodstove he planned to install in the kitchen. There would be no more fuel boat filling the tank for the generator. The wind generator, modest as it was, would provide enough light for the cottage and workshop, and perhaps sufficient heat for winter carving in his new room. He would make more members for his growing family, working by day without interruption, sleeping by night as human beings were intended to do. Also, he would make more little boats, more small puffins and cormorants, perhaps a seagull or two. Maybe he would sell one now and then, though he could not imagine how, and the thought of it filled him with aversion.

As day followed day, week after week, month after month, his routine duties continued as before, though now he spent longer hours in his shop. His original family continued to gaze affectionately upon him as he worked, though an aunt and uncle and cousin had been added. The shelves became a crowded harbor of handsome little boats, with much variety of design and color, the colors growing more flamboyant as the fires latent in paint pushed back the weather's dull overcast and whiteout. He fastidiously rendered the details—stitching the red, blue, and white triangles of linen sailcloth onto their rigging and booms. Tapping black pin nails around the rim of the decks for rail posts. Bending thick copper wire to make anchors. Gluing red and green glass beads, representing lights.

There were some whimsical experiments, making laughter into visible shapes—a circular puffin dance, the birds kicking their webbed feet left and right and flinging various wing postures; a smiling Elsie carrying a platter heaped with food. He also completed another father carrying a boy on his shoulders, much like the earlier one, but in this second version the child had his hands on the father's forehead, their eyes wide open, both of them grinning. This was followed by a lumberjack bending beneath a heavy log balanced on one shoulder as he climbed a hill. Then a lighthouse with a tiny keeper waving from the catwalk. It was a lot accomplished in one year, which he attributed to his growing sureness of hand and eye.

That winter was longer than any other he had experienced, with unusually heavy snowfall to accompany the ferocious winds. Even as it drew towards its end, it battered the coast with a series of severe storms, one of extraordinary power that threatened to crack the blades of his wind turbine. For the first time the cove froze over, though the *Puffin* was spared from being crushed by ice, as he had winched her up onto the beach before the worst blows, following a premonition.

Worried about the weather's effect on ships and boats out there on the deep, he sat in the watch room during the hours between the lowering dark of midafternoons until fitful dawns, sleeping little if at all. The beacon did not fail, though there were alarming flickers of the light that had no discernible cause. Loose wiring, he suspected, or it could be the generator's fuel pipe on the brink of freezing, the diesel too sluggish to flow. It was uncommonly cold, and the wind perilously increased the chill factor. He was often up and down the tower stairs, warming the pipe with a blowtorch, carrying replacement bulbs to the third floor, in case the beacon blew its light.

Day after day the storm worsened. Monitoring the VHF and shortwave, he heard the airwaves carrying a lot of chatter, and on the distress frequency the *Pan, Pan, Pan* messages from Coast Guard stations were now calling all boats to make as fast as they could to harbors in the Gulf of Saint Lawrence.

Despite the cove's relative shelter it was hit hard by the elements, and when the ice broke up and was hurled away westward, Ethan took the precaution of counterwinching the *Puffin* back into the water, in case he might need her. There was too much turbulence to take her out to the buoy, so he left her nose a yard from shore, tethered to a spike in the rocks, her anchor chain tight off the stern. She butted around, rising and falling and swinging wide at times, dragging the anchor a little, straining the bowline, but everything held. She would ride it out.

Each night, he made official entries in the logbook, read his books, and lightly dozed, intermittently startled awake by a blast of wind or a squawk from the radio. From time to time he jotted down thoughts in his private notebook, mainly describing the gravity of the storm, so that he might remember it clearly. It would help him recount to visitors next summer just how bad it had been. He would describe it to Catherine, maybe. And to Ross.

Though he had long abandoned any thought of writing to Ross about their bond, he still composed letters in his mind. And on a certain night in the midst of the storm's vortex, he entered one in his notebook:

Ross:

How can you accept my shame and sorrow for leaving you alone? I did not know of your existence. Now, all these years later, I would reach back across the years and try to be for you what I then could not be—if life would allow it, but it does not. I was alone then. I was a boy far younger than you are now, confused and uncertain

179

of survival. It was hard labors that steadied me, anchored me—simple tasks, learning things, and seeing wonders that showed me more than I could understand. I sought skills and I made things, a bird, a woman, a family of people who did not leave me. I made from wood and color the creatures that might have been but were not.

I thought they were enough for me. They hid from my eyes the agony of loss, the absence of a greater making—the creation of a new human being, a person who at first was not there in the world, and then who was there.

Of a child.

Of you.

He wrote more, explaining everything, even as he thought he would tear the pages from the notebook and burn them in the spring.

Deep into his watch, he was interrupted by a voice crackling out of the radio, tuned to the VHF emergency distress channel:

"Mayday, Mayday, Mayday!" came faintly through the static.

Ethan pushed aside his notebook.

He fine-tuned the frequency, and the voice came through more clearly.

"Mayday, Mayday, Mayday! This is *Petrel, Petrel, Petrel.* Over."

"*Petrel,* this is the lighthouse at Brendan's Harbour," Ethan shouted into the microphone. "What is your location? Over."

"We're the *Petrel* out of Port aux Basques in New-foundland, bound for North Sydney."

"Where are you now? Over."

"I don't know. We've been blown off course, taking on water, engine seized. The antenna mast is shattered; radar and GPS are down. We have battery lights but can't seem to raise the Coast Guard."

More static.

"*Petrel*, what was your last known position? Over."

There was no response, only crackling. Then:

"Mayday, Mayday, Mayday. This is *Petrel*, *Petrel*, *Petrel*, three-eight feet, red and white ... Port aux Basques ... preparing to abandon ship ... no dinghy ... twelve persons aboard, wearing life jackets. We're ..."

Increased static and the roaring wind made it harder to hear.

"*Petrel*, *Petrel*, *Petrel*, this is Lighthouse, Brendan's Harbour. Can you read me? Over."

"Hear you, Lighthouse."

"What was your last known position? Over."

"Last time we had a GPS connection, we were ten miles southeast of Glace Bay, but the storm's pushed us even farther south. Where are you? Over."

"About twenty-five miles south of Glace Bay. Will attempt to locate a nearby vessel to assist you. Stand by. Over."

There was no reply.

Ethan signed off and immediately called the Coast Guard. He told them what he knew and learned that the closest cutter was thirty miles northwest of Sydney, rescuing survivors adrift in a dinghy from a boat that had foundered off the Bird Islands. It would take them three hours at least to reach the *Petrel*, if they could find her—more likely four, even five.

He broadcast a general distress call to any nearby vessels, but there was no response. He tried again, and was on the verge of giving up when harsh crackling erupted from the shortwave speaker.

"Lighthouse, Lighthouse, Lighthouse, this is *Petrel*. Over," came faintly through the static.

"*Petrel*, this is Lighthouse. Nearest Coastguard vessel three to five hours away. I'm coming to get you. Over."

"How long?"

"It may be an hour, possibly two. It depends on how far east you are. Can you hold on till I get there? Over."

"We're shipping a lot of water, but we're afloat and hand pumping."

The transmission was fading, fading.

"Do you have flares?" Ethan yelled into the microphone.

"A box of flares and a gun."

It was impossible to know if the captain of the *Petrel* had completed transmission, since he sometimes said *Over* and sometimes forgot to use it.

"Fire one now," Ethan persisted, in the hope that he was not being blocked by an ongoing message. "Then keep firing every fifteen minutes after that. With luck I might be able to see you. Over."

There was no answer, not even a faint *Wilco*, "will comply". Ethan could only hope they had received his instructions.

He waited five minutes, standing at the watch room window, peering out at the heaving ocean through the rain-spattered glass. The breakers were the worst he had seen, smashing into the cliff with roaring booms, soaring upward and coating the high side of the island with freezing spray. He checked his wristwatch and saw that it was now past four in the morning. Counting the minutes, he strained for any glow that might appear on the horizon, but there was none.

Hastening down the tower stairs, Ethan tried to narrow the possibilities of where the *Petrel* might be. He knew that, at best, a boat's radio could reach only twenty nautical miles, twenty-three regular miles. Factoring in the mountainous waves, its range would be less, which meant that the *Petrel* might be relatively close to the lighthouse. And judging by what its captain had said, it was probably east or a little northeast of the island, closer to him than to any stretch of shore.

As he hastily donned his foul-weather gear and rubber boots, he knew that the flares would be crucial for locating the foundering boat. It might be anywhere within a hundred square miles or more, but if the captain kept firing the gun at continuous intervals, even a glow of light beyond the horizon would help show the way.

He grabbed a life vest from the shed and trotted down to the cove. There, after securing his vest, he waded out to the *Puffin* and clambered over her stern. Slipping under her canopy, he unclasped the canvas manhole by the outboard. That done, he fired the motor and left it rumbling in idle as he pulled up the anchor chain. The wind tried to smash the boat against the quay, but Ethan quickly revved the engine and brought her facing out into the open bay. Within seconds he was underway. Circling wide around the island in order to avoid the breakers, he soon had her rising up and over the first of a series of high rolling waves.

Now he regretted that he had neglected to install proper lights, neither green to starboard nor red to port, and no top lantern. He had been planning to buy them on his next visit to the chandlery but had put it off too long. Thankfully, days earlier, fearing the possibility of a night voyage, he had installed two powerful LED flashlights, clamped to the cabin dashboard, directing their beams ahead through the window. It was an amateur affair, but it would have to suffice.

He had a smaller flashlight with him, and with this he was able to see the needle on his pocket compass. Slowly, steadily, he made way into the east-northeast, constantly checking the black sky ahead. The farthest view was from the wave crests, but still no light appeared. In the troughs between waves, he felt himself squeezed mercilessly between black hills, pitching downward into darkness only to see the bow climbing again. Esau's motor steadfastly labored onward.

The wind howled, and bow spray beat unceasingly against Ethan's face and chest. Looking back once, he noted that the lighthouse beacon could no longer be seen, though it threw a pulsating glow against the low-hanging overcast behind him. He worried that he could easily miss the *Petrel*'s flare if he had gone too far south or too far north. Checking his wristwatch, he learned that he had left the island forty minutes ago.

Where were they?

"Come on, come on," he pleaded with her crew, "fire it, fire it, fire it!"

Frantic now, and losing hope, he was about to risk a change of course that would have brought him due east, leaving him more vulnerable to broadside pitch and roll. Before he made the fateful choice, however, a small red-orange glow suddenly appeared off the right of the bow, a light reflecting on the underside of cloud. It disappeared behind the crest of a wave and then appeared again.

Ethan eased the boat in its direction, and cranked the motor to full throttle. Again the glow appeared, larger now, with a burning coal suspended in the sky before slowly falling into the sea. Within half an hour he could see the next flare's full arc, and below it a boat's hull briefly illuminated. Ten minutes later, he was coming up on her, and saw human figures waving frantically from the deck. The *Petrel*'s hull was low in the water and listing.

Ethan brought the *Puffin* alongside her. Both boats rose and descended unequally, which made the transfer of passengers difficult. Ethan threw a rope, as did a man from the rear deck, and then they were uneasily yoked by the two cables. Ethan unfastened the *Puffin*'s canopy and began pulling it aside, but a gust caught it and ripped it all off, hurling it up and away out of sight. The man—the captain, Ethan supposed—helped two children get across the ropes, the children wide-eyed with fright but making no cries. Then came three women. One fell into the sea, but she was wearing a vest and clung to a rope, enabling Ethan to pull her from the water. Once in the boat, the women scrambled forward, packing themselves and the children under the shelter of the tiny deckhouse.

Five men came last, tumbling into the boat's open well, sprawling and clamping their hands on the gunwales for stability. This left two men on board: the captain and another.

The *Puffin* was now lower in the water, rocking and bucking, banging her hull against the *Petrel*.

"Get going!" the captain shouted against the roaring wind. "Get them to land."

"We can make it with everyone," Ethan shouted back. But even as he said it, he understood the terrible optimism of it, saw how low the gunwales were, how much spray was pouring into the well.

"No way!" the captain bellowed. "Push off now! It's their only chance."

"Where's your dinghy?"

"Lost. The wind tore it off the davits hours ago."

"All right, I'll go. But I'm coming back. Now that I know where you are, it won't take as long. Give me an hour and a half, maybe a bit more. Can you hold on?"

The man threw up his arms, giving no answer.

"How many flares do you have left?" Ethan called as he untied the rope holding the *Puffin* to the *Petrel*.

"We're running out, just a few left. I'll fire off the first, forty-five minutes from now. Then one every ten, fifteen minutes after. If she goes down ..."

The captain did not finish the sentence.

"If your boat sinks," Ethan called, "cling to some wreckage if you can. Your life vests should keep you afloat, and I'll find you."

It was then that Ethan noticed the second man, who stood quietly beside the captain. He was wearing no vest.

As the *Puffin* slid away on the downslope of a wave, he mouthed and pointed:

"Your vest! Put on your vest!"

The man shook his head.

"No more left!" the captain yelled across the widening gap. "Now go, go!"

In an instant, Ethan unclasped his own vest and threw it across to the men on the boat. One of them caught it. Waiting no longer, Ethan throttled up the motor and made the boat arc around in a half circle. With a final check of his compass, he roared off into the range of mountainous waves in the southwest.

Though the wind was now at their backs, the boat responded sluggishly. She was slower too, but their luck held, as the course kept the bow into the waves, with no broadsides threatening to capsize her and, so far, no breaking waves crashing down upon them from behind. The men bailed with the empty coffee cans that Ethan kept aboard. It seemed of little help, but it maintained morale.

Half an hour later, he spotted the pulsating glow of the lighthouse on the starboard side. Again checking the compass, he saw that the weather had pushed them a little off course, but this was easily corrected. Soon the beacon was flashing in their eyes, and less than an hour after leaving the *Petrel*, the boat entered the island's cove. The adults went over the side into waist-deep water. Two men lifted the children out and carried them toward shore. As they waded through the surf, Ethan pointed his flashlight at the gravel path.

"Go up to the cottage beside the tower," he called. "Get warm and find something to eat."

Above the roar of wind and waves, Ethan shouted as they struggled onto shore:

"Throw me a vest!"

But they could not hear him. Once again he shouted, but the survivors were concentrating on helping each other out of the waves and onto the path. Now the *Puffin* was heaving too close to the quay, and the *Petrel* did not have much time left. Every second counted. Without waiting for a reply, he reversed the *Puffin* into the bay, swung her around, and went full throttle back onto the open sea.

Without passengers, the boat was lighter, taking the troughs and crests with greater poise, though Ethan worried about the protests that came from her, the intermittent creaks and cracks and the constant groaning of tormented wood. The sky was growing pale, which meant that dawn was near. The wave height was noticeably lower though still treacherous, the wavelength from crest to crest growing wider. Yet the boat's canopy was gone, and she was taking on water. The wind, too, was full in Ethan's face, the spray stinging his eyes.

He hoped that the *Petrel* would stay afloat long enough for him to reach her, for life vest or not, a man immersed in the North Atlantic at this time of year would last no longer than minutes. He would freeze to death before he drowned.

Now time was the fluid dimension, stretching longer and longer, confounding his every glance at his wristwatch. No flares appeared in the sky ahead. Then, finally, he spotted a fading glow in the east—south-southeast according to the compass. He altered his course toward it. Shortly after, another appeared, though it was no brighter than the first. The *Puffin* was making less headway, due to the change of angle across the waves, and she was taking on more water, the bilge washing forward and backward around his ankles as she rose and fell and rose again.

On and on it went, and the motor never failed.

Ethan wondered why there were no more lights, and he concluded that the *Petrel*'s captain had run out of flares. It seemed as if hours had passed when finally he spotted a larger ship crossing his course, heading northwest, a mile or so away. All her running lights were on, with bridge and portholes shining against the charcoal sky. Seeing her flag, he recognized a Coast Guard cutter.

Was she searching for the *Petrel*?

He had no time to think more on this, because now he could see in the grey light of dawn a red-hulled boat just ahead of him, fully rolled over and wallowing in the seas—her keel and propeller lifting as she went down by the bow.

Ethan throttled lower and slowly approached, his flashlight scanning the immediate waves for survivors floating nearby. Risking his own boat, he circled widely around the wreck, crossing the waves abeam, rolling and righting, but finding no survivors. As he watched, the *Petrel* went under and disappeared.

He tried to signal the cutter with his flashlight, hoping to call her back. Someone on deck must have spotted him, because she gave three short toots on her horn, though she continued to accelerate away. The ship's loudspeaker cut in, but all he could hear above the roaring wind was the metallic squawking of disconnected words:

"... two crew ... safe ... *Petrel* ... return to port ..."

Now Ethan understood. The last of the *Petrel*'s crew had been rescued.

Nevertheless, on the off chance that he had not understood correctly, he made two widening circles around the bubbling point where the boat had gone down. On the final circuit, the *Puffin* tipped dangerously close to a roll from which there could be no recovery, but Ethan swung the motor hard to the left and brought her out of it. With a sigh of relief, and deft maneuvering, he guided the bow back toward the west and headed for home.

During the following minutes the run toward the coast continued as expected. The sun must have risen by now, for the entire ocean was a writhing mass of silver beneath the overcast, and yet Ethan saw by its light that the waves were again growing higher. The wind had risen above forty knots, for the waves were developing overhanging crests, and more and more foam was blown off into spray. The boat was being driven before a savage tailwind, and the waves were climbing from ten feet in height to what looked like twelve and fourteen before they collapsed upon themselves. Exceeding a third of the boat's length, they had the weight and potential power to knock her down into a trough from which she could not arise.

Now it was a race against time and chance, for the wind and waves were moving faster than the boat, even as the *Puffin* went slower and slower. The motor was as brave as ever, but the hull grew ever more sluggish with the bilge water sloshing against Ethan's shins. To stop and bail would be a futile effort.

Then came the very thing Ethan had dreaded. Though he did not see it, a massive wave arose behind him, sixteen or eighteen feet high, with a hanging crest, and then it collapsed full force upon the *Puffin*, just as a freak crosswind twisted her and pushed her into a roll. Combined, the two forces cracked her hull and drove her under.

Stunned, Ethan desperately lashed his arms and legs, trying to swim, trying to surface. The wave passed, and within seconds he was gulping for breath, surrounded by fragments of the boat.

Ethan clung to the wreckage, his limbs quickly numbing. The next wave lifted him high and tossed him, further battering his fractured ribs, every breath draining his last reserve of energy, great painful gasps that took in spray-filled air and a greater amount of icy saltwater, which he coughed out, only to have his mouth fill again. The weight of his body was pulling him under now, his fingers frozen, gripping the remnant of the craft that would no longer save him.

So this is the way I will die.

The next wave, higher than the ones before, lifted him up and up and up.

And now I die alone.

These were his last thoughts, for the wave peaked and hurled him into a black ravine, breaking him.

As his body sank, Ethan looked downward into the abyss as the darkness rose to take him. Yet in his final conscious moments, he lifted his head once more and gazed upward, his arms rising, reaching for light. And then he saw a man coming toward him, walking on the water, telling him not to be afraid. And a woman was beside the man, her face compassionate and wise, her arms reaching to Ethan to enfold him.

The Sentinel

In the aftermath of the storm, efforts were made to find the lighthouse keeper's body. It was never found, nor did any identifiable wreckage from his boat wash up on the beaches of Nova Scotia.

On the day after Ethan's death, Ross Campbell was struggling to come fully awake over a cup of coffee, in the kitchen of his family's home in Halifax. His mother was making breakfast and listening to the radio.

The newscaster described the damage caused by the storm, the two sea rescues, and a single casualty, the loss of a lighthouse keeper at Brendan's Harbour. The keeper was named.

"Oh, no," Ross groaned, scraping back his chair and standing abruptly.

"What's the matter?" his mother asked.

"Oh no, oh no," the boy repeated. He began pacing around the room. "It's the man I stayed with last summer. He's drowned."

His mother gave him a look of sympathy.

"I'm sorry, Ross," she said. "That's a real tragedy. But you didn't know him very well, did you, dear?"

Ross dropped his eyes and left the room. He grabbed his jacket and headed swiftly out of the house. He walked through the city streets until he came to a lighthouse tower on a hill overlooking the harbor. There he stood for a long while, gazing out to sea.

On that same day, Catherine MacInnis sat eating lunch in a coffee shop in Toronto, a city where she had been hired as a pianist with a symphony orchestra. A television in a corner of the café was broadcasting news of the storm in the Maritimes, with video footage of ravaged coastal towns and interviews with survivors of two rescues. When Ethan's name was mentioned as a missing lighthouse keeper involved in one of the rescues, Catherine began to cry silently.

"He gave me his life vest," said a survivor, choking up. "I'd have drowned without it. I think he's gone."

That evening, at Massey Hall, Catherine played Rachmaninoff's Piano Concerto no. 2 in C Minor. She played it as she had never played it before.

For you, Ethan. This is for you.

When she had completed the concerto, she rested her hands on her lap, closed her eyes, bowed her head, and thought of him, while the audience rose to its feet and erupted into unceasing applause, like the sound of the sea, of waves that bear tidings from a distant shore.

Elsie Whitty heard the news on the radio, and wept, and clung to hope, and in the end she grieved. She often prayed for Ethan's soul and had Masses offered at Saint Brendan's. Whenever she looked up at the ship hanging above the center aisle, she saw her husband Norbert at the helm, but now Ethan stood beside him.

Late in the summer, a man dropped into her B and B, asking for supper and a room for the night. He was black, with a funny accent, not North American. As she served him his meal, he asked her if she had ever met a man named Ethan McQuarry, the lighthouse keeper who was lost during the great storm.

With damp eyes, Elsie said yes, she had met him. Knew him well, in fact.

"A prince of the sea," she said.

"I think so too," the man replied. "I'm the fellow he rescued, the last one on board the night the *Petrel* sank. He gave me his life vest."

Elsie sat down across the table from him, openly weeping now, trying to dry her eyes with the hem of her apron.

"He sacrificed his life for me," the man said.

She nodded and nodded, and gave up trying to find a reply.

"I wanted to see where he was from," said the man. "I'm hiring a boat to take me out to his island."

"The island's open, sure enough," said Elsie. "I hear the tower and his cottage are locked up until the legal business is settled."

"Then I will walk upon his island and try to imagine his life."

"Where are you from?" she asked at last, to keep things moving along.

"Nigeria. I have been studying in Canada, and I hope to be ordained a priest next month."

"Oh," said Elsie and reached out, placing her small hands over his big ebony ones. "I'm glad for you."

His African warmth seemed at ease with this intimacy of strangers, and did not withdraw. He pondered her toil-worn hands, spotted and wrinkled, and thought of his own mother. And before the eyes of his heart there passed the countless souls he would serve in the years to come, the weddings and funerals and baptisms, the confessions and counsel, and his own loneliness and joys that would bear eternal fruit. And he thought of the drowned man who had made it possible.

Eight months after the *Puffin* went down, on a day of bright sun and frothing surf, an old man and a little girl walked hand in hand along a white sandy beach in north-eastern Brazil. It was not far from their village, which was hidden behind the dunes. No tourist ever came there.

The old man was ninety years old, bent and wizened under a lifetime of sun and adversities. His skin was brown, his hair white. Though he lacked teeth, his smile was warm. He was known by all in the village, and in his large extended family, as Esteban. The little girl, his great-granddaughter, was named Maria Esperança o Espírito Santo de Frias.

Esteban was content to shuffle along, enjoying the cool wind and the presence of the girl, who was the light of his heart. From time to time she broke away, running ahead barefoot in the wet sand, splashing her feet in the curling surf and dampening the hems of her ragged pink dress, then coming back to him to seize his hand and make their arms swing. Though it hurt his joints he made no complaint.

They were about to turn around and go home when Maria spotted something flashing on the lip of the surf where it touched the beach. She ran to it and bent over to pick it up. It filled her arms, and she walked slowly back to the old man to show it to him.

"Look, *bisavô*, it is a bird!" she cried.

"Do not touch dead birds, Maria," he scolded.

"But it is living!"

She held it out to him.

"*Ai, ai*, it is a wooden bird," he said. Looking closely, he marveled. "Yes, it is the *papagaio-do-mar*, the sea parrot, cut from a tree and painted."

"Oh, I am sad that the colors have fallen away."

"Some color remains, and the wood is without harm."

"Yes, it is so pretty, so pretty," she crooned, holding the bird close to her chest, rocking it as if it were a baby.

Etseban sat down on the sand, for his legs were weary. And as the girl walked back and forth along the edge of the water, cradling the bird and singing to it, he thought about her.

Oh, I see now how you will be, what you will become. You will be beautiful, and I will love you always.

In the spring of the year after Ethan's death, a boat beached in the cove of Lighthouse Island. The tide was going out, the causeway exposed. Though the day was cool, the sky was lightly brushed with high clouds, the sun radiating its mild April light.

Two visitors stepped out onto the sand, Ross Campbell and his wife Rachel, who was carrying in her sling their newborn child.

"It's hard to believe this place is ours," said the woman. "It seems a bit unreal."

"Oh, the island's very real," he said with a smile as he guided their way up the gravel path toward the tower. "More real than many places we've been."

"Yes, I can feel it too. I see why you loved it here, Ross, why you're always talking about it."

"I wasn't here long, but they were happy hours."

"I still don't understand why he left it to you in his will. Do you think he had a premonition of death?"

"No, I don't think it was that. He was young, probably thought he had years of life ahead of him."

"But why you?"

"I simply don't know. The lawyer says Ethan never explained."

"Oh, it's magnificent!" his wife cried as they approached the tower. "Is it still in operation?"

"Not anymore. They hired a temporary keeper after Ethan was lost, but he's no longer needed now. The automated beacon above Brendan's Harbour came online last autumn."

"Mmm, but a machine isn't a sentinel, is it?"

"Too true."

"It needs a real sentinel, a watchman with eyes and heart."

Ross jangled a ring of keys. "Do you want to see inside the tower first?"

"I think *you* want to see inside the tower first," she said with a laugh, squeezing his arm. "As for me, I'd love to see the cottage."

Thus, after unlocking the cottage, they went in.

The place smelled of must and damp. Daylight came poorly through the dusty kitchen window.

"It's primitive," Ross said with an apologetic tone.

"It's wonderful," said Rachel.

"Wait till you see the designer outhouse."

"Can't wait."

She sat down on a wooden chair and began to nurse the baby. Ross flicked the switch for the ceiling light, the one connected to the wind generator. It glowed brightly.

"Yay, it's working!" he said.

When the baby was full, cooing and trying to keep drowsy eyes open, Ross said, "Come on, I want to show you something."

He led her through the pantry and opened the door to Ethan's carving room. Going in, he turned on the light and stepped to one side.

The look on Rachel's face was worth waiting for. He had wanted to tell her about the carvings, and how fine they were, but had held back, wishing to surprise her.

"Oh, Ross," she breathed, her eyes wide with amazement.

"I know."

"He made them all?"

"Yes, he did."

She spent a long time inspecting each one, savoring them.

"There's a spectrum of sad and whimsical here," she said with something like reverence. "But most of all there's beauty."

"All this came out of a quiet man, Rachel, a small man. Some would say an insignificant man."

"There's no such thing," she said with a shake of her head. "You're not going to sell these, are you, Ross?"

"There's rather a lot of them. You'd need a fair-size home to display them tastefully and not make it look like a tourist shop or an art gallery."

"But they already have a home," she said with a musing tone, and he looked at her.

Later they unlocked the tower door and climbed the stairs to the watch room. Excited by the view through the window, Rachel could not stop looking. Using the telescope, she scanned the vista from north to southwest.

"A whale," she said. "I think I see a whale."

"It probably is." He looked through the scope. "Yup, it's a whale. He's looking at you."

"Ha!"

"There to the north, see the little black speck," said Ross. "That's Wreck Isle. Now over here, on the other side, you can see the new lighthouse."

So it went for a time, and then he showed her the beacon's clockworks and the radios.

"It looks like the temporary keeper left everything the way he found it," said Ross, flipping through a logbook.

Rachel wandered over to the chart table and paused to look at a stack of thin notebooks on the shelf beside it. She opened one and turned a page.

"These must be Ethan's private thoughts," she said. "Notes about seashells and birds. A poem or two."

She flipped another page. "Storm descriptions, ideas, and what looks like a draft for a letter ..."

"How about I make you a traditional lighthouse supper, fresh out of cans?" said Ross. "We'll open a bottle of wine, and I'll tell you some stories about him. And then we can read his journals together."

"Sounds good," she said, closing the notebook. "Maybe I'll get to know him a little, after all."

They walked to the edge of the island, facing the sea. He showed her the puffin nests, and she pointed out silver seals sporting in the surf. They stood close to one another, Ross's arm around his wife, the baby asleep in her arms. The breakers pounded the rocks below, sending up fountains of spray, roaring and yet somehow comforting.

"This is a place where we all could live," said Rachel.

Ross smiled to himself. "Ethan will love it here."

Together, they gazed down at their child. He was awake now, with his pink face and wisps of golden hair feathering in the breeze, the apple cheeks and blue eyes, the smile that said he was grateful for existence. He was looking at his parents, very happy to know them.

"I'm glad your friend's name was Ethan," said Rachel. "But I think I would have named the baby Ethan even if we'd never heard of your lighthouse keeper."

"He was a steadfast man," said Ross, placing his hand on the boy's head. "I hope our son will be like that."

"He will be, if he's anything like his dad."

They held each other closer, gazing out at the horizon, watching the ocean heave its tide against the shore, feeling the course through the heavens of their small planet, an island in the infinite sea.

And the sea gave up the dead that were in it; and death and hell delivered up the dead that were in them: and they were judged, every man, according to their works.

—Revelation 20:13

AUTHOR'S NOTE

There are more than forty lighthouses in operation on the coasts of Nova Scotia, many of them now automated. The island and lighthouse and nearby port in this story are fictional. The puffins are quite real, and several of the human characters, though I should say that the marvelous people of Cape Breton are more varied and colorful than these few representatives imply. Novels, like telescopes, try vainly to reduce an ocean into a little space.